HER RIGHTEOUS PROTECTOR

NIGHT STORM, BOOK EIGHT

CAITLYN O'LEARY

© Copyright 2021 Caitlyn O'Leary
All rights reserved.
All cover art and logo © Copyright 2021
By Passionately Kind Publishing Inc.
Cover by Lori Jackson Design
Edited by Rebecca Hodgkins
Content Edited by Trenda Lundin
Cover Photo Courtesy of Reggie Deanching/RplusMphoto.com

All rights reserved. No part of this book may be reproduced in any form or by any electronic or mechanical means, including information storage and retrieval systems—except in the case of brief quotations embodied in critical articles or reviews—without permission in writing from the author.

This book is a work of fiction. The names, characters, and places portrayed in this book are entirely products of the author's imagination or used fictitiously. Any resemblance to actual events, locales or persons, living or dead, is entirely coincidental and not intended by the author.

The unauthorized reproduction or distribution of this copyrighted work is illegal. Criminal copyright infringement, including infringement without monetary gain, is investigated by the FBI and is punishable by up to five years in federal prison and a fine of $250,000.

If you find any eBooks being sold or shared illegally, please contact the author at Caitlyn@CaitlynOLeary.com.

This is the last book in the Night Storm Series.... For now. I might follow up with a team member at a later time, who knows? But I do want to take the time to thank the four people who have stuck with me when I have been a child, a mess, a terror, and hell to work with during this series. Drue, Trenda, Rebecca, and my husband John have cared for me, been patient with me, supported me, and showered me with both tough love and kindness. I could not have published these books without them.

SYNOPSIS

Navy SEAL Lieutenant Max Hogan has watched as every single one of his men has paired off. He is beginning to wonder if there is something more to life than just mission after mission.

He is surprised the moment he's asked to attend the reading of a will and even more surprised when he discovers who has passed away. He was sad this woman he'd had a brief relationship with was dead, but he hadn't seen her for five years, so why in the world would he be sitting in her lawyer's office?

Ten minutes later Max is staring at the man, uncomprehending. The lawyer's words don't make any sense. His lips continue to move, but all Max keeps hearing is that first sentence.

"Megan wanted you to have custody of your son if anything ever happened to her."

He has a son?

Once centered around endless missions and keeping his men safe, Max's life is about to change in ways he never expected. Can he rise to this unexpected challenge, and will he have to do it alone? Or will his son's guardian turn out to be his closest ally—and more?

1

MAX HOGAN SMILED AS HE PULLED HIS BLACK SILVERADO truck into his driveway. His lawn had been mowed, which meant he owed Mikey some money. Getting a chance to see his neighbor always put a smile on his face; he never knew where their conversations would end up going and he loved that. He hit the garage door opener to get into his house, and satisfaction flowed through his veins as he saw his baby. He really wasn't that surprised to see that the cloth cover on his 1969 Mercury Cougar was out of place. Mikey was as much of a car guy as he was, and when he'd put back Max's lawnmower he could never resist looking at or sitting behind the wheel of Max's restored car.

When he got into his house, he turned on the air conditioning then peeled out of his fatigues, and hit the shower. He and his team had done a lot of physical training today, and even though he'd showered at the base, he still wanted another one. When he bought the nineteen-fifties house seven years ago he'd planned to fix it up, but the only thing he'd ever worked on was the bathroom. He'd taken out the bedroom closet so that he could enlarge the bathroom, which allowed for a spa-sized shower and bathtub. It was his oasis. Other than that, the small three-bedroom, two-bathroom house was just a place to lay his head down between missions. Oh yeah, he'd added air conditioning—living in Virginia, that was a necessity.

When he got done with his shower and put on a T-shirt and cargo shorts, he called Lester Sinclair, Mikey's father. Lester answered on the first ring.

"Hi, Max. Feel like some home cooking?"

Max winced as he remembered the last meal that Lester had made. It had been damn near impossible to chew the rump roast that he'd cooked into shoe leather. "You don't have to go to any trouble. I was planning on Pollard's for some chicken. How does that sound?" Max asked.

"Sounds great, but only if you let me pay," the older man said.

"Normally that would be great, but I won a bet with Cullen today. He thought he could beat me on the obstacle course. He lost. I've got cash burning a hole in my pocket."

Lester let out a hearty laugh. "Well, if we're eating on Cullen's dime, let's go for it. You know what Mikey and I like. Come on over."

"I should be there in about a half-hour."

"Sounds good."

Max picked up the keys on his counter, plus the Hot Wheels model that he'd bought last weekend, and left his house. He moved his truck to the street, then locked it. It was a perfect night for a drive in the convertible; what's more, Mikey would love a ride. He drove over to Pollard's and put in an order for twenty pieces of chicken, mashed potatoes, hush puppies, coleslaw, corn on the cob, fried okra, cinnamon apples, green beans, and homemade corn muffins. He knew that Lester was on a tight budget so this should last a while. Max made a mental note to give Cullen a heads up before he saw Lester again, to let him know about all the bets he'd supposedly lost.

When he parked the Cougar on the street in front of the Sinclairs' house he wasn't surprised in the least to see Mikey out front waiting for him. The big man's grin was a sight for sore eyes.

"Max! Max! Max! I mowed your grass! Did you see? Did you?"

He was practically jumping up and down with excitement.

He ran down the walkway and gripped the side of Max's car.

"I can help carry in dinner? Did you get hush puppies? Them's my favorite."

"I did," Max assured Mikey. He handed him one of the bags, then hit the button to bring the top up so he could lock the car while he was inside with Mikey and Lester. By the time he walked up to the door, Mikey had the screen door open, waiting for him.

"I got your mail today, too!"

Max grinned at Mikey's exuberance. Everything the man said was an exclamation. How could anyone be unhappy when they were around someone so filled with joy?

"Mikey, don't block the door and let Max in, the food is getting cold."

"I'm not, Dad, I'm helping." Max handed Mikey another sack of food and followed him to the kitchen table. Lester had already started to unload the containers of food.

"What did you do, buy out the entire restaurant?" Lester asked.

"I was hungry and everything looked good," Max explained. He dumped the last bag onto the table and went to the cupboard to get the plates, then grabbed the silverware they were going to need. When he was done he reached into the fridge and found the ever-present pitcher of sweet iced tea. He might spend a lot of time over at his friends' and teammates' homes, but if he had to say where he felt most comfortable, it was with Lester and Mikey.

When they got settled down at the table, Mikey grabbed their hands. "Can I say Grace?" he asked.

"Of course," Lester answered.

"Bless us, oh Lord, and these thy guests for the bounty for which we are about to receive, thank you, Amen. And thanks for a whole bunch of food from Max, especially the hush puppies."

Lester and Max laughed, then they all started to fill their plates.

"Mikey, you need to eat some of those green beans before you have another hush puppy," his father said kindly. Mikey rolled his eyes but did as he said.

"Can I go for a ride in your car tonight?" Mikey asked Max, even though his mouth was full. This time Lester rolled his eyes. Despite the fact that Mikey was almost fifty years old, he had the mental capacity of a seven-year-old. Lester had explained to Max that his umbilical cord had wrapped around his neck and deprived him of oxygen, so he hadn't developed like other children. Lester was now seventy-nine years old and living on social security and what the VA paid him due to a back injury he suffered during his service in his twenties. Lester had been talking to Max about options for Mikey when Lester passed on, and he had some ideas, but Max hoped that would be a long way off.

"I was hoping you'd want to take a ride with me, Mikey," Max smiled.

"But don't forget to give him his mail," Lester reminded his son.

"Oh yeah." He started to get up from the table.

"Not yet," Lester smiled. "Finish your dinner first."

Mikey set his plate back down and started to shovel food into his mouth at a rapid pace, anxious to get Max his mail and then go for a ride. Again, Max was overwhelmed at the man's joy with his world.

Soon the food was all put away.

"Are you sure you don't want any to take home?" Lester asked for the third time.

"You know how it goes," Max said. "I never know when I'll have to leave. I don't want leftovers that will just go to waste."

Lester nodded.

Max turned around when Mikey slapped a pile of mail onto the table, as usual, it was a mound of junk mail. But there was one unique difference—a Federal Express envelope on the top of the pile.

"What's this?"

"I found it on your porch," Mikey explained. "It's mail, isn't it?"

"Yep," Max agreed. He turned it over and saw that it was from a law firm in Chicago. When he opened it up he found just one piece of paper inside. It was a letter.

Hmmm.
He sat down at the table to read it.

Mr. Hogan,

I wish to apologize for the tardiness of this letter, but it took some time to locate you. I will be brief. You have been named as a beneficiary in the last will and testament of Meghan Todd. It is of utmost urgency that you respond and attend a reading in person. Please contact me personally at your earliest convenience.

Respectfully Yours,

Elias Peterson
  Attorney At Law

Max pulled his phone out of the pocket of his cargo pants and called the attorney's office. It was no surprise that it went to voicemail, so he left a message. What did surprise and frustrate him was that there wasn't a mobile number or an e-mail address.

"What was that all about?" Lester asked.

Max scratched his chin. "Beats me. Supposedly I was left something in this woman's will, but I've never heard of her."

Lester gave him a hard look. "That is strange. Are you sure about that?"

"Absolutely."

"Can we ride in your car now?" Mikey interrupted.

Max turned to the man and grinned. "Let's get going before it gets dark." He shoved the letter and all the mail into the FedEx envelope and scooped it up to take it with him to the car. Then he remembered his present for Mikey.

He stood up and pulled the Hot Wheels car out of his pocket. "I bought this for you." He handed the yellow Corvette to the man and watched his eyes go wide.

"It's awesome. I don't have a yellow one. I've got to put it on my shelf." He ran to his bedroom.

Lester glanced down at the floor, then back up at Max. "Max, you really didn't need to buy so much food."

"Lester, it's like I told you, I wanted to taste a little bit of everything."

Lester shrugged and smiled. "Well, son, Mikey and I appreciate it."

When Mikey came back Max pulled out the twenty-dollar bill that he always gave the man for mowing his yard.

"Dad, I have more money, do you see? Is this a lot?"

"It sure is," Lester gave a wry smile and shook his head at Max. "As usual, it's too much, now go put it in your piggy bank."

"Okay." Mikey pounded back down the hallway.

"You're too good to him," Lester said to Max.

"That's just not possible to be too good to your son. You and Mikey have made me feel like part of your family, you know that." Max looked around the mid-century house, with its faded sunflower wallpaper on the kitchen walls, and smiled. It reminded him of the best foster home he had ever lived in when he was a child. There had been a child with Down's syndrome who'd made him feel welcome and wanted; he had hated having to leave that house.

Mikey came running back to the kitchen table.

"I'm ready!"

Max laughed. "Well, let's get going."

WHEN MAX GOT HOME, he sat on his couch with a beer and re-read the letter. It made no sense; not only did he not recognize Meghan's name, but he'd never been to Chicago. He didn't want to wait until tomorrow for answers, so he grabbed his cell phone off of the coffee table. His second in command answered on the second ring.

"Hey, Max, what's going on? We're still on standby, right?" Kane McNamara asked.

"It's not official yet, but yeah," Max answered.

"Thought so. I'm staying at the condo in Virginia Beach this weekend, not going out to Lake Anna. Even though it's not official, I trust your instincts, Lieutenant."

Max heard the grin in his friend's voice. "I appreciate that, Kane. But I got to tell you this is your friend Max calling for a favor, none of this lieutenant bullshit for the moment."

Kane laughed.

"You know I'll do anything you need, Max, whether it's professional or personal. Do you need me to hide a body?"

"Nah, if I needed a body hidden I would have called Cullen."

"I'm hurt. What's more, you're thinking is wrong.

Cullen might be able to come up with an ingenious way to hide the body, but I'm not a hundred percent sure he could keep his mouth shut," Kane chuckled.

"When push comes to shove, all of the team could be trusted," Max said with confidence. "And lucky for me, this favor doesn't include a dead body."

"Okay, what do you need?" Max liked how serious Kane sounded.

"I need you to get some information for me. I'm forwarding a picture of a letter I received and I want you to get as much information as you can for me. Apparently, I've been named as a beneficiary in some woman's will, but I've never heard of her. I really don't want to wait until Monday to find out what this is all about, especially when we could be going wheels up this weekend."

"Are you sure this isn't from a Nigerian prince?" Kane joked.

Not bothering to respond, Max texted the picture.

"Hmmm, it looks legit," Kane finally said. "I'm surprised there isn't an e-mail address attached."

"So was I. When I went online, I found a listing for the law firm, but no website, which was also pretty odd. The attorney is a member of the American Bar Association, and it looks like he's been practicing for at least forty years."

"That might explain why there isn't a website," Kane commented. "Maybe he's really old-school and depends on word of mouth."

Max sighed as he swirled the beer in the bottom of the bottle and looked out his window. "Could be, but I want a heads up on what the hell is going on."

"Do you think this could have something to do with one of the foster families you lived with?" Kane asked.

"That's what I've been thinking, but seriously, Kane, most of them didn't have a pot to piss in. They were relying on their checks from the state. What's more, I was raised in Minnesota, and the law firm is in Chicago. Nope, nothing is computing."

"Okay. I'll have something for you tomorrow," Kane promised.

Max heaved a sigh of relief; he hated mysteries.

"Thanks, man."

"It's nothing."

"How's A.J.?"

"Her latest project has her in knots so she's spending a lot of time in Atlanta," Kane said. Max could hear the frustration in Kane's voice. He knew that his friend supported his wife's career as a television producer, but he also wanted to spend as much time as possible with her.

"Can't Python take over?"

"Paul," Kane said. "Remember, he likes to be called Paul now. No, he can't. Right now it's taking A.J.'s magic touch. But I'm picking her up from the airport tonight."

"Well hell, Kane, then I can't ask you to do this for me. I'll get Gideon from Omega Sky or Dex from Black Dawn to help me out."

"Fuck that noise," Kane said emphatically. "You're mine and I'm yours. The day you start seeing other computer guys is the day I divorce you, you got that?"

Max laughed. "Yeah, I got it. I take it A.J. has a late flight, huh?"

"Yeah, she does," Kane admitted. "Otherwise I'd tell you to piss up a rope. There is no way I'd be giving up my quality time with my wife."

"Thanks, Kane, I appreciate it." Max was still chuckling as he hung up his phone. The thing was, he knew his friend and second in command was a master of multi-tasking. He'd seen him run programs inside of programs and still run a marathon at the same time. He'd come up with something for Max by morning.

Now he could sleep in peace.

2

The phone jarred Max awake. It was the ringtone that told him it was coming from his commander. He grabbed it off his nightstand.

"Hogan," Max answered.

"The mission is on," Commander Clark said without preamble. "Get your team to base, I'll start the briefing in an hour."

"Got it."

"Max?"

It wasn't often Max had heard that tone in Simon's voice, so he knew he wasn't going to like what was coming next.

"Yeah?"

"This is going to be a tough one."

"Aren't they all?" Max asked as he rolled out of bed and grabbed a pair of pants out of his dresser.

"This one is going to be different. You're going to have a fight on your hands and it's going to hurt. But I trust you to get it done."

"Simon, what are you talking about? We're going in

after the missing reporter, right? The one who's been targeted by the head of the Taliban?"

"Yeah, but I heard from one of my contacts she's entrenched. But I don't give a damn, you and your team have to get her the hell out of there before this becomes an international public relations nightmare."

Max winced. "How high up has this gotten?"

"You don't want to know," Simon sighed.

Max's hand hesitated over his gun safe. "You're right, I probably don't, but unfortunately I do."

"I told you to quit watching the news, it'll rot your brain," his commander said with a wry laugh.

"This is Lark Sorensen we're talking about right? Her mother's the CEO of InTechno. No wonder this could turn into a political clusterfuck." Max pulled out his gun and then grabbed his body armor out of his closet. "Okay, I'll get the team rousted. We'll be on base in less than thirty."

"Even Kane? Thought he takes off to Lake Anna every weekend."

There it was, one of the reasons that Max liked his commander; he took the time to know the men who reported under him.

"I talked to my men on Wednesday and told them to stay close, I felt like something was brewing."

"Well, you were right. I'll see you in the briefing room closest to my office when you get here."

Simon hung up and Max pulled up the group text for his SEAL team. In one quick blast, he told them all to immediately get to base and expect to head out for an unknown length of time.

Within sixty seconds every man on his team responded in the affirmative, and by that time Max was in his truck. When he pulled into base parking, the competitive part of him was a little perturbed to see that Asher and Raiden had already arrived.

How in the hell did Raiden arrive first when he lives farther away?

Max stopped thinking about it and started focusing on the fact that Asher made a decent pot of coffee as he made his way down the corridor to the briefing room. He grinned when he saw his oversized mug placed on the front table with steam rising out of it. He glanced over at Asher and smiled.

"Raiden, how did you—" Max started to ask as he lifted his mug of coffee.

"Gabriella left for a Wyoming tour on Thursday, so I was over at my parents' today to replace their storm windows. Figured since we were on standby I might as well stay there since it was closer to base."

Max nodded as he took his second sip of coffee. The three men in the room turned as Cullen Lyons and Zed Zaragoza walked into the room.

"Who made the coffee?" Cullen immediately asked as he headed to the coffee pot. "Please say it wasn't you, Max."

"It was Asher."

"There is a God." Cullen turned over two mugs and emptied the carafe for himself and Zed. "Asher, you're going to have to make another pot for the others," he said as he wagged the empty container up in the air.

Max looked down at his watch. Seven more minutes and it would be the thirty minutes he had allotted for everyone to reach base. He wanted to give his men as much info as he could before the commander came in. He knew that Commander Clark would still be here to go over everything.

Kane slipped in the door, dropped his gear, then dropped down into a seat and started scrolling through his computer tablet.

Typical.

Ezio, Leo, and Nic were the last two to arrive. Max waited until everyone had a mug of coffee before he leaned against the desk at the front of the room. He looked over his men with a sense of satisfaction. Nobody could ask for a better team. Nobody.

"So it's back to the sandbox," he announced casually.

"Sounds great to me." Leo lifted his mug with a grin. "I'm pretty damn sick of the rain."

"And the dark," Zed piped up.

"Which country?" Kane asked, never looking up from his tablet.

"Afghanistan," Max answered.

Kane's head shot up. All eyes were now looking at him. Even Cullen managed to look serious for a moment.

"Commander Clark will be here pretty soon to give us all of the details. He said this will be tricky."

"Does that mean he thinks some of our assignments have been easy?" Asher asked.

"No," Simon said as he entered the room. "None of your missions have ever been easy in my opinion. They might have been a little heavy in the romance department," he chuckled. "But never easy."

"Hell, I'm here to tell you, the romance part was the hardest part," Zed said laconically.

"You got that right," was Kane's dry agreement.

Everybody nodded in agreement. How in the hell so many of his men managed to fall in love with women they'd met while on missions still amazed him.

"You all realize that we have a shitstorm on our hands

if I'm the one coming in to brief you," Simoon said. "This isn't because I think this is tougher than your normal mission—hell you'll come through with flying colors—it's because this is a major political clusterfuck and I'm going to need constant updates."

Simon sent Max a sideways look of apology.

"There's a reporter by the name of Lark Sorensen who was last seen in Kandahar. Her mother is Beatrice Allen, the founder of InTechno. Your job is to get her the hell out of Afghanistan."

Jesus, no wonder the situation's so explosive.

Max looked around at his men. He could see that every one of them understood how consequential their target was.

"You've got it," Max said.

Simon handed Max the file he had been holding, then turned to Kane. "Max will give you the passwords you'll need to get into the encrypted server to get all of the details that we currently have. All communication reports will be going directly to myself and Captain Hale. He would have been here, but he's currently in-flight from Coronado."

"Understood," Kane nodded.

"I want a report as soon as you determine your point of entry," Simon said as he looked at Max.

"You've got it." He nodded to his commander.

He watched as Simon left the room, then turned to his team. "Start loading up your gear while Kane sets up everything we need to go over." He turned back to Kane. "How long will you need?"

Kane didn't bother looking up. "Less than ten minutes."

"You heard him," Max said. "Get back here in less than

ten minutes."

He watched as his men filed out. Max went over to Kane's gear and found the pouch that contained Kane's prized mini projector. He plopped it down on the desk in front of him. "Does this thing connect with your tablet?"

Finally, Kane looked up from his tablet.

"You didn't just ask me that, did you?" he mocked. "What decade are you living in? If things weren't originally made to adapt wirelessly, then there are usually ways to make them adapt. If you can't, you get something new. With me around, things adapt."

"You're sounding kind of pompous, you know that, don't you?"

Kane ignored him as he continued to work on his tablet. Max watched with admiration as he saw that Kane was actually putting things into a presentation format. Max shook his head and headed for the door.

"Max, wait up a second."

"Yeah?"

"I've got some info on your girl." Max frowned for a moment, then realized Kane was talking about the will.

"Yeah?"

"Yeah. I'll tell you on the plane."

"Sounds good." Max left for his office. He knew that Kane would get them the information they needed, but he wanted to do a little bit of research on Lark Sorensen while he had the time. When he pushed open the door to his cramped office he was surprised to see Kostya Barona sitting in one of his two visitor's chairs. He looked tense. Max closed his door and sat down at his desk.

"Kostya, didn't your team just get back from Central America on Wednesday? What are you doing here?" he asked the big, blond lieutenant of Omega Sky.

"I know what your assignment is," Kostya said bluntly.

Max managed not to react. He knew damn good and well that Simon had this situation on lock-down, so how in the holy fuck did Kostya know what was going on?

"Look, Max," Kostya started. He was sitting with his knees apart and his hands clenched together between them; he was definitely tense. "I'm not going to tell you how I know, but I do. What I am going to ask...plead... with you, is to take me with you on your assignment."

Max kept his features blank; he had no choice. He knew how Kostya had gotten his information. It was the same way that he always got his information, and that was from his second in command, the man who handled all of his team's communications and commuter intel, Gideon Smith. But what reason did Kostya have for wanting to get involved with Lark Sorensen's rescue?

"Kostya, I've known you for four years. We've been on three missions together, and I would literally trust you with my life. But this?" Max raised his eyebrow. "You're going to have to give me more."

Kostya swallowed down a sigh. "I know. I know." He stood up in the small room. "Max, I know that you and your men have done what you could to support the men and women who aided you during your time in Afghanistan."

Max nodded. Nobody talked about it outside their own teams, but it was something that definitely went on. They had done what they could for those people who had risked their lives again and again for them over the years to make their country better.

"That's true," Max agreed. "But what does that have to do with Ms. Sorensen?"

"The reason she wasn't evacuated with everyone else was that she wouldn't leave Ebrahem Nuri's family."

"Nuri?" Max pictured a short man that he had met once in the middle of the night outside of Kabul. He had provided some necessary intel that had been critical to his team, then had disappeared into the darkness.

"You mean Ebrahem didn't make it out of Kabul? Didn't he and his family get Special Immigrant Visas?"

Kostya's expression turned bitter. "He was killed before he could apply, and by the time his wife and kid's visas finally got approved there was no way for them to get out of the country. Max, that man is the reason four of my men are alive today. I won't turn my back on his family. I can't."

Max couldn't imagine what he would do if he were in Kostya's shoes. He thanked God that his team's assets had all made it safely out of Afghanistan.

"Have you talked to Simon?" he finally asked.

"You know he wouldn't allow it. This is your op."

It was true.

"How good is your intel that the Nuri family is with Ms. Sorensen?" Max asked.

"It's golden," Kostya assured him.

Fuck. Well, he wasn't a special forces lieutenant for nothing. It was his job to make quick decisions. He'd come up with some reason why it was critical to have Kostya on this mission... At least by the time they got to Afghanistan.

"Get your shit, then meet up in the briefing room."

MOST OF HIS team had gotten some shut-eye during the flight from Virginia to Souda Bay in Greece, even Kostya. They all knew that they would need it. Max watched as they all unbuckled themselves from their jump seats and stretched.

"I've been in touch with the base commander," Max called out. "We're going to leave all of our weapons in the armory here on Crete. The last leg of our trip will be a commercial flight from the UAE to Pakistan, so there isn't going to be a way for us to take our weapons with us. All of our other gear will be fine."

The plane door opened, and a middle-aged bald man appeared at the top of the steps. "Lieutenant Hogan?" he asked.

"That's me," Max stepped forward.

The man stepped into the plane. "I'm Commander Andino," he said with a thick Greek accent. "I'll show your men around."

"How long before we'll be ready to depart for the UAE?" Max asked.

The commander looked down at his watch. "No more than two hours. Hopefully a lot sooner. I'll show you where the mess is, and where the armory is." His tone was no-nonsense.

Max nodded. "I appreciate it. A couple of us have a few things we need to finish up, then we'll find you, will that be all right?"

"Of course." He looked at the rest of Max's team who had stood up. "Please follow me."

Kane kept his seat, staring at his screen and planning on making a report to Simon, while Zed was the last one out of the plane. Max watched him carefully. He'd been off disability for a year, but his injury had been life-threatening, and even though Zed was one of the biggest and strongest men on his team, Max still watched out for him. He turned his attention to Kane.

"Whatchya got?"

"Based on the intel that the CIA has provided, it looks like the last known location of Ms. Sorensen was in Kandahar, which was one of the last government-occupied territories, so that makes sense."

"Did you take in the info I texted you about Ebrahem Nuri?"

Kane nodded. "Both his parents and his wife's parents were from Sangin, so that's likely where she ended up after he was killed."

Max nodded. "Okay, Kane, then this is it. We're going to explain that Kostya is onboard because he has info on the Nuri family, and he's been in contact with Ms. Sorenson. Can you backdate some communication between Kostya and Lark to back this up, so when the Commander informs the CIA it's bulletproof?"

Kane winced. "No can do, not when I'm in the air, and not with the equipment I have here. We're going to have to pull in someone else."

Max raised an eyebrow. "Gideon?"

Kane nodded.

"Do you have some ideas on how it can get done, and what we need?"

"Give me five minutes to let them percolate, and with Gideon involved they should be boiling before we leave Crete." He grinned.

"Okay, let's get out of here and grab Kostya. Then we'll get on the phone with Gideon. But before we do, make sure you take care of yourself in the meantime."

Kane stood up and turned to the door, then paused.

"Max? I have some info on this Meghan woman from the will that I think will shed some light on things."

Max shook his head. "Not interested right now, we have bigger fish to fry."

Kane nodded, and they both headed out of the plane.

3

BEFORE THEY GOT BACK ONTO THE PLANE, MAX USED HIS own computer to compose an update to Simon explaining the next steps of their mission. They were headed to Al Dhafra, the military airport on the eastern coast of UAE. From there, they were going to take a commercial flight into the Quetta International airport in Pakistan, which was two hundred and forty kilometers from Kandahar in Afghanistan. Recently, Pakistan had been turning a blind eye to the American military's presence in their country, despite their leader's official stance. Additionally, the Chaman border crossing had just re-opened the previous week due to economic pressures from both countries, so that would make it much easier for them to figure out a way to get into Afghanistan from Pakistan.

They were going to be met at the airport by three expats, one American and two Brits. The American was a former Army Ranger, both of the Brits were former SAS. He and Kane would be communicating with them during their flight and formulating a plan to get them over the Pakistani border and onto Kandahar. Max didn't mention anything about Kostya at that point; he wanted to ensure that Gideon worked his magic to provide a backstory so that he and Kostya had a decent reason for him to have snagged a ride-along with Max's Night Storm team.

By the time Max got back onto the plane, Simon had acknowledged receipt of Max's communique. Now for the hard part—ensuring they had two fucking workable plans in the hours it would take to get to the UAE. Kostya had changed seats and was now on one side of Kane while Max was on the other side.

Max had worked with Roger Snyder before. The former Army Ranger major was a good man. Smart. He'd married a Pakistani woman almost twenty-five years ago. They had lived most of their married life in the UK, and their children had been educated there, but his wife's mother had become ill so they came back to live near her. As for the others, the only thing Max knew about them was through mutual friends. He hoped like hell they could supply the firepower and transportation they were going to need.

Kostya and Kane were already working with Gideon, figuring out scenarios on how to explain Kostya's presence on the mission.

And it better be fucking good!

Max sucked in a deep breath.

Calm, Hogan. Calm.

With Kane working things out, it would be a marvel, he assured himself. It was time to worry about how in the hell they were going to get over the Pakistani border and then past all the Taliban checkpoints in Afghanistan. Max texted Roger so that they could talk. He wanted a plan in place as soon as they landed in the UAE since they weren't going to be able to formulate one when they were on the last leg of their trip. Max was also hoping like hell the CIA would have some intel as to where Ms. Sorensen was currently located.

While he waited for the call back from Roger, he perused his team. He couldn't help but grin when he saw that Leo was reading a book. This time it was *Lost Horizon* by James Hilton, pretty apropos considering the fact they were headed back to Afghanistan. Next, he saw that Asher and Raiden were both leaning in to hear whatever load of bullshit Cullen was spewing, and it must have been good, going by the grins on their faces.

Zed was thumbing through his phone. If Max had to guess, he was looking at pictures of his wife and the cutest kid imaginable, and that would be his daughter Lulu. She had to be almost three years old now. Ezio and Nic were both getting some shut-eye. Max's phone vibrated; it was Roger.

"Yeah?"

"Max? I've got Nigel and Randall with me. Have you got your flight arranged yet into Quetta?"

"Yep. We'll be arriving at fourteen hundred hours on Monday. We'll be coming in on UE150. We need weapons; we have our gear, but everything else we had to leave in Crete. First, is it possible for you to get your hands on what we'll need? Second, how can I get you the list in a secure fashion?"

Somebody laughed, Max couldn't determine who.

"That's bloody funny. I've heard about your gun shows in the States, but they wouldn't hold a candle to what's going on over here. Since the US pulled out, every day has been like a bloody arms swap meet."

"If you know the right person, that is," Roger said. "Max, text me the list on my phone, and we'll get you everything you need. But I know you SEAL types and how damn picky you are, so it won't be by Monday, it will probably take until Wednesday. Which will help us get the transportation arrangements finalized."

"So you have an idea on how we're going to get to Kandahar?"

Max had talked to Mason Gault, who was the lieutenant of Midnight Delta. He and his team had done an intense rescue two days after Kabul had fallen. They'd needed to get a group of eight relief workers out of Kunduz who'd been trying to assist Afghans with dual citizenship to successfully leave the country, but they'd been caught up by the Taliban. Mason had been able to give Max some suggestions on how he and his men had been able to use both ambulances and civilian vehicles to smuggle their team and the relief workers to the airport in Kabul. They'd needed to switch up their mode of transportation at the drop of a hat at least four times, and at one checkpoint there had been a real problem.

Mason told Max how two of his men, Finn Crandall and Drake Avery, had handled the situation. After watching just how violent the men at the checkpoint were to the people preceding them, Mason knew there was no way that they were going to have a chance of getting past. Drake and Finn traded one of their vehicles for two motorcycles. They broke the long line and sped past the checkpoint, shooting at the Taliban members as they went. All of the guards took off after them. Leaving the post empty for everyone else to start going through the checkpoint.

It had been a daring move by the men of Midnight Delta, but it was a calculated risk. Both men were trained snipers, and as soon as they were on higher ground they jumped off the bikes and aimed at the jeeps coming toward them. They blew the tires out in seconds, which left the Taliban members sitting ducks, all the while the relief workers and the rest of Midnight Delta made it past the checkpoint. All of the Taliban soldiers had been killed.

Mason went on to explain how they'd handled the rest of the rescue operation to get the relief workers on one of the last planes out of Kabul, so he supplied enough ideas that Max felt comfortable collaborating with the team in Pakistan.

"My wife's cousin does some welding as a side job. I've hired him to supervise building some metal crates for wild boars. Nobody has blinked an eye at the request," Roger said.

"Meanwhile, I've spent a shit-ton of your American money, Mate." Again, Max had no idea if it was Nigel or Randall talking.

"How'd you do that?" Max asked.

"I just purchased three flatbed trucks. We're going to be transporting over a thousand bags of plaster into Afghanistan. Perfectly reasonable, because the Taliban is wanting to show what do-gooders they are, re-building everything they just blew up." Max could hear the derision in the man's voice.

"That's where the metal crates come in," Roger said. "You're all going to be inside the crates, surrounded by the bags of plaster. It's going to be miserable as fuck, but it will work. Nigel has worked it out on the Afghan side; there are real buyers for the material, so we shouldn't run into too many problems with paperwork."

Max just thanked God it was November when the

temperatures normally didn't get up past sixty degrees Fahrenheit.

"This is Randall," Randall said.

"Appreciate the clarification," Max said.

"Thought you might. Anyway, the way we see it, there might be times we can let you *wild boars* out of your cages for respite, but that'll have to be under the cover of night."

"Understood. So, all of you are really sure that you can get us the weapons we'll need?" Max asked again.

"Max, just text in your order; it'll be like putting in a take-out order to McDonald's. I'll bet you one hundred dollars we won't even have to do any substitutions," Roger said with extreme confidence.

Max liked the sound of that.

"And another thing—I'm Nigel by the way—we have the nine of you booked into three different hotels. We need to pick you up at different times and go different routes to get to the trucks."

"Ten. There's ten of us now," Max said. "I'll text you with his passport information."

"Is there a problem?" Roger asked.

"No problem, just a change in plans."

"Okay. This number is safe to send and receive calls and texts. I'll get you the room information before you land in Quetta. Each group will be met for their respective hotels at the airport."

"Thanks, Roger," Max said.

"You're welcome."

The line went dead and Max turned his attention to Kane and Kostya. Kane looked up and gave him a quick nod. Max relaxed. He leaned back so he could start thinking about his report to his commander and wondered just how hot the blowback about Kostya was going to be.

BY THE TIME they landed in Pakistan, Max had his answer. Simon was *not* happy. Before sending his formal report when they set down in the UAE, he had called his commander, wanting to give him a heads-up.

"This phone call is the only thing saving your ass—you understand that, don't you, Hogan?" Simon Clark growled.

Ezio picked up Max's gear as they headed to the truck that would take them to the side of the airport for commercial take-offs.

"I do, Commander."

"So this thing with Kostya, just how much of it will stand up when the brass and men in suits start picking it apart?" Simon asked.

"It's as good as gold."

There was a long pause. "In other words, Kane has done his magic, and maybe Gideon was involved," Simon sighed. "But cut to the chase for me, Max. How goddamned vital was it that Lieutenant Barona flew his happy ass along with your team on this mission?"

"After hearing everything the lieutenant had to say, I determined his presence is critical."

"Okay then. Send in your report, you have my full backing."

Max got onto the truck with the rest of his men and then took his seat next to Kane. "You can send the report off to Commander Clark and Captain Hale," he told Kane.

He watched as his second in command pulled up a file on his tablet and pressed a button.

"Done," he smiled at Max. "Now do you want to know what I found out about the reading of the will?"

"Now's as good a time as any."

"Does the name Meghan Lancaster or Meggie Lancaster mean anything to you? She used to live in Tennessee."

Max's eyes widened. The only friend he'd held onto from his foster care days had been James Rockfield. He'd attended Jimmy's wedding five years ago in Tennessee. It had been a week-long affair, because Jimmy's bride-to-be had wanted all the trimmings. Rehearsal dinners, combined bachelor and bachelorette parties, combined baby shower, the works. The way Loretta put it, she and Jimmy's friends and families lived far and wide, and this would probably be the only time they'd ever be in one place at one time again, so she was making the most of it.

Max had been one of Jimmy's groomsmen, and Meggie Lancaster had been one of Loretta's bridesmaids. There'd been an air of vulnerability about her that had brought out Max's protective instincts the first moment he saw her. It hadn't been necessary for Jimmy to tell him that Meggie had been hurt by her newly ex-husband; it showed. Nevertheless, Meggie had come onto Max all the same, and by the second night of her not-so-subtle hints, Max had given in. Even now, five years later, he smiled thinking about that woman. She'd told him that he had helped her to heal, but he'd never understood why she'd then gone on to ghost him for the next year, until he'd finally given up. Now, to hear that she'd died felt like a gut punch.

"Max? Max? Are you all right?"

Max looked up at Kane. "No. No, I'm not. I remember Meggie, I just can't believe she's dead."

Kane's eyes glittered with compassion as he waited.

Max knew his friend had more to say, but it was taking a few moments for him to wrap his head around the fact that the lovely woman he had made love to in Tennessee was no longer alive.

"You ready for the rest?" Kane asked.

Max nodded.

"Her divorce was finalized three weeks after the wedding. Three weeks after that, she moved to Chicago where she took out a restraining order on her ex and changed back to her maiden name."

Max hadn't realized that her divorce hadn't been finalized, but he'd had a damn good idea about the abuse she'd been put through, so in his mind, she was definitely a free woman when they'd been together five years ago.

"Anything else?" Max asked.

Kane nodded and put his hand on Max's shoulder, and squeezed. "Yeah, there is. Seven months after she moved to Chicago she had a son with the father's name left blank on the birth certificate."

Chills raced down Max's spine. His eyes widened as he looked at Kane. "He can't be mine, Kane. Not only did we use protection, but the woman I knew is not someone who would've kept my son a secret from me. She just wouldn't have."

Would she have?

Kane gave a swift nod. "Okay, we'll go with that. Then what do you think is going on?"

"That bastard she'd been married to, he was sick. The abuse ran deep. It's possible that he impregnated her and that's why there's no father listed."

Kane nodded again. "And the reason you're in her will?"

"You mean to tell me you haven't hacked into this guy's server yet and found it?"

Kane grimaced. "This guy, Elias Peterson? He's been practicing since Clarence Darrow. I think he probably wrote this will with a quill pen. The law firm doesn't have a website. He has an AOL e-mail address and I can't find a server in their office," Kane said with disgust.

Max chuckled. "This must be killing you."

"It is."

Max laughed louder when he saw his friend's teeth grit together.

"Good, you needed a worthwhile challenge. Not everything in the world can be conquered via the computer, young man. Now figure something out."

The truck stopped and Max and his team got out so that they could climb up the stairs onto the commercial flight to Quetta, Pakistan.

4

MAX STARED UP AT THE CEILING FAN IN THE HOTEL BEDROOM and tried to fall asleep. They'd gotten in really late, so Kostya had checked in with Gideon and Jase who were on his team, and then fallen asleep, but Max hadn't had such luck. He kept circling back to Meggie Todd. Scratch that, Meghan Lancaster. It had bugged the hell out of him that he couldn't get a total picture of her in his brain. It didn't seem right. He remembered her blonde hair, but not the exact shade. Were her eyes hazel, blue, or green?

He picked up his phone off the nightstand and pulled up Jimmy's social media site so he could pull up some of his wedding photos; hopefully, Meggie's picture would be there. It didn't seem right that he couldn't clearly remember how this woman looked. As soon as he went back through Jimmy's photos, he found what he was looking for. There she was, two women to the right of Loretta. Meggie.

What a sweet smile.

Max sucked in a deep breath. He zoomed in on the picture.

Her eyes were blue. Then he saw the dimples on either side of her mouth. How could he have forgotten those? Sweet. She'd been sweet. He'd always wondered what she would be like when she finally got her feet under herself. When she got back the confidence that her bastard of a husband had taken away from her. Max had had a faint idea of what she'd once been like, and a hope of what she could be like in the future. He'd even toyed with the thought of being part of her future, but she hadn't been interested. All in all, he hadn't been that surprised she'd shied away from any kind of continuation with him. Besides the emotional and physical blows she'd suffered from her husband, she'd made a reference to being estranged from her parents. Meggie hadn't had a lot of trust left in her; hopefully, that hadn't transferred onto her son.

"Max?"

Max kept his eyes on the fan and answered Kostya. "Yeah."

"You're thinking too loud, it's disturbing my rest."

Max chuckled.

"Is it the mission, or are you dropping by the wayside too?"

Max turned his head on the pillow so he could see Kostya's form on the other twin bed in the hotel room. "What do you mean by the wayside?"

"Hell, even when I let you take Ezio for a few missions, your team managed to corrupt him and he went and fell in love. What is wrong with your team?"

Max heard the sincerity in the other lieutenant's voice. This time he didn't chuckle.

"So falling in love is a bad thing?"

"It is for men like us," Kostya answered. "We're not

made for a soft life to share with women. That's not who we are."

This was interesting. "So you're saying we don't have feelings?"

"Max, don't hand me that black and white shit, you know that isn't what I'm saying. We couldn't do what we do without having compassion and feelings. I'm saying that we put our lives at risk too often to put a family through that kind of emotional rollercoaster."

"Is that what Ezio has done by pairing up with Samantha? Seems to me that she was the one putting *her* life at risk."

Max waited for a response.

"That is one scary lady. Fearless and scary. Ezio is going to have his hands full for the rest of his life." Kostya's voice was filled with admiration.

"Ah, so maybe it's not all so bad."

"That brings us back full circle to my question of why you're thinking so hard."

"Tell me more about Ebrahem's family," Max asked.

"I can take a hint." Max heard a smile in Kostya's voice. Good, he wasn't insulted that Max wasn't in sharing mode. "Ebrahem showed me his kid's pictures a couple of times. Both little girls. The way I figure it, the oldest can't be more than eight years old. He told me that there wouldn't be a chance in hell he'd be doing the kind of work he was doing without his wife's total backing. Her mother and aunt had been killed by Taliban members, as well as Ebrahem's father's family. They were both committed to bringing a better way of life for their daughters."

"It's about time you told me who your sources are who told you about the Nuri family and Lark Sorensen. I'm assuming that the stuff that Kane and Gideon fed the brass is all bullshit, right?"

"Right," Kostya said. "If I told anyone who my source was, it would blow things up."

"Well, we're all here, so it can't blow up anything now. Who's your source?"

"Lark Sorensen."

Max sat up and swung around, his feet hitting the side of the bed. "What?"

"Lark. She's aware of who her mother is and that she'd be extricated. She also knew that anybody who came in after her would not give two shits about the Nuri family; their marching orders would be to get Lark home, and that would be it."

Max's shoulders shifted. Kostya must have seen it in the moonlight.

"Max, you don't have to tell me one way or the other, but I'm positive that your marching orders are to get Lark out of there and nothing else, that's it. She knew it, that's why she grilled Samira Nuri to find out the names of American military that her husband trusted, and then Lark got ahold of me. I'll be damned if she didn't track down my cell phone number and call me. I swear, she has a Gideon-like person on her payroll," he said with pride. "I would bet that it's somebody who works in her mother's company."

"So she got you on board with saving the Nuri family. I get it."

"Max, this leaves you and your team free to do what you need to do to carry out your primary mission to get Lark out of Afghanistan. You can leave the Nuri family to me."

Max snorted. "I told you, Ebrahem worked with me and my guys too. I'm on board with this, Kostya."

"You won't be if you have to make an either-or decision," Kostya warned.

"Then it's up to you and me to make sure there aren't any 'either-or decisions'. Where is Lark now? The CIA has told us Kandahar."

"When she called me she was in Sangin. That's where Samira Nuri's parents lived, but she said it wasn't safe there, and they would be moving on. I haven't heard one damn thing from her since I was in your office back in Virginia."

"Dammit," Max bit out.

"I was going to say something worse," Kostya admitted.

"What's your gut say?" Max asked the man.

"I sure as hell wouldn't count Lark Sorensen out. What's more, I've decided to put my faith in a God who wouldn't rain any more tragedy down on the Nuri family, so I say they're safe someplace. I expect Lark to reach out to me again."

"Or maybe the CIA will get us something."

"Stranger things have been known to happen." Max heard the smirk in Kostya's voice.

"Wild boar, huh? Did I ever tell you about the time that we went huntin' for wild boars? My cousin Freddy took me and two other cousins with him out near Abilene. I was fifteen," Cullen started his story. Nigel and Randall were enthralled, but Max walked away; he was sure that somehow the story was going to end up with Cullen making a pet out of a baby boar, or wrestling an alligator, and he didn't have time to hear it. He wanted to know the status of the weapons.

He walked to the back of the shop, past the welders and blacksmiths to the foundry, and found Roger talking to the foreman. He tilted his chin and Roger followed him out the back door. When they were out of earshot, Max asked Roger what the status of the weapons was.

"It's only Tuesday," Roger said. "I told you that you would have everything by Wednesday."

Max gave the former Army Ranger a hard look; he really didn't appreciate his lackadaisical attitude. Roger held up his hands to soothe Max.

"Seriously, Max, everything's on schedule."

"Do you mean to tell me that everything on the list is coming at one time? That doesn't make any sense."

"No, some of it has already arrived," Roger said.

What the hell?

"Then I want to see it."

"I don't have it, my guy Mohammed has it. He's coordinating everything for me."

"Roger, a lot of cash has exchanged hands. I would have thought that by now we'd have something to show for it. I want to see what Mohammed has."

Roger pulled his pack of cigarettes out of his vest pocket and once again searched all of his other pockets for a matchbook. Max felt, then saw Kane come out the door and step up beside him. "You talking about the weapons?" he asked.

Roger lit his cigarette.

"Yes," Max answered.

Roger pulled out his mobile phone, pressed a number, and started speaking in Arabic. He was going fast, but

Max kept up. He doubted that Roger had any idea that Max knew the language as well as he did. The man hung up and continued to look at his phone, then he slid over to Max.

"Here, scroll through the pictures." Max saw the ten Sig Sauer p226s, ten Ka-Bar knives, not his first choice, but they'd do. There were eight AK-47s and two M4A1s. Then there were the four MP7s but no M240s. Max also saw that the four MK13 sniper rifles weren't there, and the grenade launcher that was there wasn't worth a damn.

"Tell him to get those to us today. We need to make sure they're in working order. I want my men to feel comfortable with them now. Also, I want two decent grenade launchers, not that China shit."

Roger nodded as he took back his phone. "I'll make sure you get the stuff he has in the next hour, and you'll get the rest by dawn tomorrow."

Max nodded, then went back into the workshop. He walked over to Cullen who was done bullshitting, thank the good Lord. "Whatcha got?" he asked the man.

"I looked over the purchase orders from the Afghan Construction company. I used a translation app, they look good. They even have a high-ranking Taliban signature for the receipt of the plaster. Nigel did a great job pulling this off; I think we should make it through the checkpoints. What I'm worried about is some kind of plan to get us back out of Afghanistan, but he's saying he has some ideas."

Max looked over at the Brit who was in the shop office talking to the owner.

"What about Randall, what has he got going for us?"

"He's delivering on all the plaster and the trucks. They're supposed to be here tomorrow morning, bright and early. I'd say the real problem is getting all of us over here from the hotels without drawing attention to ourselves. But I have a plan, and it's sneaky."

Max chuckled. "Does it include alligators?"

"And sparklers," Cullen grinned. "You got to throw them off the scent. But seriously, this will work." Cullen got a funny look on his face.

"When will you give me a run-down?"

"I'll have it to you in an hour. Just want to talk to Asher; I have to see if he can scrounge up something."

"What kind of wild goose chase are you sending Asher on?"

"A good one, you'll like it."

Max nodded, then moved along to talk to Kane who was wearing a welding helmet. The goddamned perfectionist was making sure that the welds were strong enough to hold. Max couldn't help grinning to himself. He picked up a welding helmet from one of the stations and tugged it on, then tapped Kane on the shoulder and motioned him back toward the foundry.

"Yeah?" Kane asked.

"Let's send out an update to Simon."

Kane jogged back to the wall by the office and picked up his backpack, then came back and took out his tablet. Max watched as he pulled up the encrypted message site, then he lifted his eyebrow.

"Update them on the mode of transport to Afghanistan. The paperwork looks pristine to get us there, it even has the Taliban's leader's cousin's signature on it, so we should be good at all the checkpoints to get us to Kandahar. Zed's Arabic is fluent, and Leo is passable and they are both dark enough to pass for natives so they're going to be two of the drivers. Randall is currently working on getting them their proper identification so they can pass border checks. Roger has highly recommended a local Pakistani for the third truck."

Kane was typing as Max was talking.

"Most of the weapons we need will be here in two hours. You and I are going to check them out to make sure they're all in good working order. The others will be here at dawn, or they damn well better be."

Kane looked up and waited for Max to continue to talk.

"Well, you talk about the cages, since you've been over there inspecting them."

Max looked over Kane's shoulder and saw him key in the description of the cages and how they would be deployed on the trucks. Kane looked up at Max.

"Anything else?"

"Tell the commander that we anticipate leaving in thirty-six hours."

Kane nodded, keyed in the info, then sent the missive.

"Well, that's done. Simon didn't give me much shit about Kostya coming, you and Gideon did a good job on the backstory. But what kind of chatter have you seen come in from the CIA? Have you been monitoring them?"

"Oh ye of little faith," Kane shook his head at Max. "Of course I have. The men in black have looked over the backdated e-mails, but they haven't found anything that's raised any kind of red flags. We know what we're doing."

Max gave Kane an arch look. "If you were such a damn hotshot, you would have gotten into that attorney's computer and found the will."

Kane narrowed his eyes. "I can't very well get into a computer that isn't connected to anything, now can I?"

"What happens when he's on the internet, can't you access him then?"

"Jesus, Max, you really think it's that easy? I've sent two e-mails with spyware to his AOL account but he hasn't clicked on them. I need him to do something like that so I can get into his computer. He's not hooked up into any kind of network that I can see. It's probably just his lonely old desktop computer that was built before the year two thousand."

"And here I thought you were the best," Max smirked.

"You're an asshole."

It was fun getting under Kane's skin, it didn't happen all that often.

"My work here is done," Max said as he sauntered away.

5

Thirty-three hours had passed since his last check-in with Simon. Max stood next to the loading dock and watched as the second truck was loaded with plaster. Nigel had arranged it so that nobody from Pakistan Gypsum was here at the warehouse, including the night watchman. It had taken a little less than an hour to load the first truck and ensure that the cage was securely hidden, but that the men could see out and had enough air coming in. The cages had been built long and narrow, so that if the Taliban were to pull out one layer of a side bag, the cage would still be concealed by another bag. Asher had worked a stint driving short-haul, so he was quick to point out the best way to load the bags of plaster so that one side could be easily dislodged between checkpoints and then quickly repacked without looking out of place.

Ali Baqri was driving the first truck, and despite Kane's epic failure with the attorney in Chicago, the man was able to come up with quite the background check on Ali.

Max had no idea how he was able to find anything, considering the fact that Ali was a citizen of Pakistan, but Kane managed it. Anyway, it confirmed Roger's advice that Ali was the right man for the job, so he was the third driver. His truck had Cullen, Asher, and Kostya in the cage. Leo would drive the truck that was being loaded. Kane and Nic were already inside the cage, all three of them armed and loaded for bear as they watched men load the bags around and above them on the flatbed truck.

Finally, it was time to load up Zed's truck. Max, Ezio, and Raiden got inside the cage. It was placed up close to the truck tractor, and then Nigel, Roger, and Randall started to load the bags of plaster. They were going to be flying blind when it came to communications; they'd already tried to see if their mics would work while they were concealed under the bags and discovered they wouldn't. Max knew that Kane must be feeling like a baby without his pacifier since he couldn't use his tablet. The only consolation was that here in Quetta they had signals on their satellite phones so they could call and text one another. Hopefully, that would continue.

"Who chose our roommates?" Raiden asked as the last bag of plaster was placed, and the three men were ensconced in darkness.

"I did," Max said.

"Why did you stick us with Ezio?" Raiden asked. "All we're going to hear about is Samantha this and Samantha that. He's been with her for over a year and he still hasn't shut up about her. What in the hell were you thinking, Max?"

Max let out a loud laugh. It was true.

"I resent that," Ezio remarked. "And, I counter with the

fact that you have been moaning about Lisa going out whitewater rafting without you, and we've been stuck looking at pictures and pretending we give a shit."

"He's got you there," Max said to Raiden. Seriously, I need to get a whole new team of bachelors."

Max was comforted to feel air coming in from the side and the top of the cage, Asher had done a great job of explaining the best way to load the bags.

The truck began to move. He looked down at his watch—it was oh-four-hundred hours. Even though A75 was a major highway and it was only one hundred and twenty-eight kilometers to the Afghan border, it was going to take them five to six hours because the trucks were so heavily loaded. The crapshoot was going to be how long they'd need to be at the checkpoint into Afghanistan.

MAX, Raiden, and Ezio were all zoned out. Maybe once every ten minutes there would be something loud enough for them to hear and comprehend, but that had been it. They'd been at the border crossing for twelve hours. If Leo wanted to get their attention about anything, he was supposed to grind the gears of the truck, so right now they were safe to rest. When they got past this checkpoint, Ali had said that there shouldn't be any more checkpoints until they got close to Kandahar, which was another one hundred and fifteen kilometers. Before they'd left Pakistan, Max received intel from Simon that there was a small distribution warehouse located on the outskirts of the city. It had suffered some light damage during the bombings, but from the aerial shots that they had, it should provide enough coverage to hide the three trucks.

Once again the truck moved forward. Was it an inch? Two inches? Leo was a good driver, no grinding of the gears.

Max grinned to himself. He'd done well not to have included Cullen on his truck with him; it was always a careful balancing act. Yeah, Cullen could entertain the hell out of you, but then there was the point where you felt like throat punching the asshole.

"Am I seeing you grinning over there, or am I hallucinating?" Ezio whispered.

"Who, me?" Raiden asked quietly.

"No, Max."

"Yeah, I have a smile on my face. I think I'm delirious." Max answered beneath his breath.

"Really?" Raiden asked.

"Okay, thinking about Kostya."

Ezio snorted. "Yeah, as Kostya's former second in command, I thought it was pretty fucking funny that you put him in the cage with Cullen. He's going to drive Kostya batshit crazy. Since English isn't Kostya's first language he isn't going to catch all the nuances of Cullen's stories, so that will piss him off. Then there's the fact that Cullen rambles. You do realize that Cullen might not make it out of his cage alive, right?"

"That's why I put Asher in with them," Max said. "He's a hell of a peacekeeper."

"Makes sense," Raiden said.

This time the truck rolled forward what felt like a meter...maybe two. Were they actually going to get over the border?

"I think—" Ezio started.

The truck's gears started to grind. All three men picked up their rifles.

Max grabbed the three-inch diameter plastic pipe that had been painted the same color as the plaster bags and shoved it between the bags, just to the first level. It wouldn't show on the outside, but it would allow them to hear better than they could without it.

"I can't give you everything. My boss said half to you, and half to the man in charge at the Kandahar checkpoint." Max had never heard Leo sound like such a kiss-ass before.

Two men started screaming at Leo, then Max heard Zed's voice.

"Have you read the name of the man who signed the paperwork?" Zed asked.

"Yes," one of the screamers screamed. "I know how much profit your boss is making selling all of this Pakistani plaster to our poor country. There is a price to be paid for crossing our border, and it will be paid."

"Give me your name." Zed's voice was low and deep. "Now!"

"You don't need my name." There was a pause. "You have no right to take my picture."

"I have been told to report anybody who holds up this transport. You are holding us up. We have set aside enough money to pay for this border crossing and money to pay to get into Kandahar. Take what it is offered, and let us across."

The fact that Zed was huge did not hurt when he was pushing back against the Taliban soldiers. He always did a good job waving the carrot and wielding the stick. It only took a minute.

"Give me the money and keep the other half for the Kandahar checkpoint," the screamer said in a normal tone of voice.

There was a normal hum of voices surrounding the truck, but Max didn't hear Leo, Zed, or the screamer anymore and then the truck started up again. When it felt like they'd progressed a kilometer, Max sighed with relief.

THEY WERE NOW in a new kind of hell. The road that they'd driven on in Pakistan had been pretty well paved, but what they were dealing with here in Afghanistan was not the same story. Max knew it was basically the same road, but it had to have been beat up during all of the fighting. Not only were there potholes, they were also clambering over clumps of asphalt. Talk about a rough ride.

"*Aaarrrggghhh*," Max gritted out as he hurled sideways into the muzzle of someone's rifle. It nailed him on his side in his ribs where he wasn't protected by body armor.

"Fuck!" Raiden was too loud.

Ezio wasn't talking.

The truck had tipped to the side, but by some freakin' miracle Leo had righted it. But for a second the damn thing had been coasting on just the wheels on the left side. Had Leo been a professional NASCAR driver?

Max tried to suck in some air, but he had trouble. Goddammit, did he break a rib? Was his lung punctured? Had the truck's tire been punctured?

"Are you two okay?" Ezio gasped. He sounded like shit.

"Ezio, what's wrong with you?" Max asked.

"Hit my head against one of the bars. I'm bleeding. I passed out for a second."

"Raiden?" Max asked the man to report about himself.

"Hit my elbow against one of the bars. It was nothing,

shouldn't have shouted out like a dumbass," he said disgustedly. "Ezio, move over here so I can check out your head wound. Lieutenant, what's your status?"

Raiden was one hundred percent into his medic mode, but Max wasn't listening. He was feeling around for the plastic pipe; he had a bad feeling that this potential wreck might not be an accident. When he touched the pipe he found that it had come loose, so he shoved it back in so that he could hear the outside world. Nothing. He heard nothing. That meant they didn't have a lot of other traffic close in front of them or behind them mulling around like they did at the checkpoint, so they were probably on the side of the road. But what was really frustrating as fuck was that Leo was not talking to them. When something like this happened, Leo should have been talking to them. This was bad. Very, very bad.

Where was his ChemLight? Every man had one thanks to Cullen talking about sparklers. Fuck, he couldn't reach his.

Max pushed the pipe further up so that it penetrated past the top layer of the plaster bags. It was risky, but he desperately needed to hear whatever the hell was going on out there. He also put his phone up near the pipe to see if it could get any kind of signal since there was an opening. One bar.

"Max, what are you doing?" Raiden asked.

"Take care of Ezio," Max responded.

"Okay."

Max heard the sound of two truck doors slamming shut. Dammit, why wasn't Leo talking? His man knew enough to talk so that they could stay informed. There was a problem. He couldn't call Leo because Max would bet his bottom dollar that he was in trouble. Max sent out a group text.

Wʜᴀᴛ's ɢᴏɪɴɢ ᴏɴ?

Iᴍᴍᴇᴅɪᴀᴛᴇʟʏ ʜᴇ ɢᴏᴛ something back from Zed.

YOUR TRUCK SHOT, LEO FORCED TO PULL OVER. TWO MEN HAVE BOARDED, SITUATION UNKNOWN.

Lᴇᴏ's ᴘʜᴏɴᴇ better have been locked; the last thing he needed was some hijacker seeing an English text. The truck started but it was tilting to the left. The bags of plaster were harnessed in pretty tightly, so Max thought they shouldn't fall off.

"How's Ezio?" Max asked Raiden quietly.

"I'm fine," Ezio answered.

"I can't get the bleeding to stop," Raiden contradicted Ezio. "In other words, you're not fine."

Max shifted and took a shallow breath. He wasn't fine either, but he wasn't going to say anything. A broken rib he could live with, but a punctured lung was a bit of a problem. "What do you have to stop the bleeding?" Max asked.

"I could use some help," Raiden admitted. "I'm jammed in here pretty tight. Do you have some wiggle room to grab your undershirt?" he asked Max.

"Move Ezio my way, then you take yours off," Max

instructed Raiden. He found his ChemLight then twisted it and the cage took on a weird neon green glow.

"Why?" both men asked simultaneously. They both knew that something was up with Max.

"I have a problem with a rib," he admitted reluctantly. "Someone's rifle caught me between my armor plates."

"Goddammit," Raiden hissed. "How's your lung? Is it punctured?"

"Breathing's not what it should be, but I could just be winded. I'm monitoring the situation," Max told him. "Ezio, crawl over to me." Max watched Ezio shift over to him, then there was a lot of rustling noises as Raiden started getting out of all of his gear.

The truck took a sharp turn and they all slid up against the right of the cage. Max heard Ezio suck in a deep breath and he felt warm liquid hit his wrist. "Hurry up with that shirt, we've got to get the bleeding stopped."

"Hell, Max, you know head wounds always bleed a lot, it never means anything," Ezio scoffed.

Ezio's face was covered in blood. He was in trouble.

Max tried to take a deep breath but failed. Max looked down at the incoming text from Zed.

GOING TO PASS LEO'S TRUCK AND FORCE IT TO STOP.

MAX KNEW that underneath the seat of each of the cabs there was a submachine gun. They were zip-tied high up so that they wouldn't be found at the checkpoints, but with the wire cutters in the glove box, they could be easily cut loose. Still, it would take a minute to do it—would Zed have that minute?

WHERE'S ALI? Max texted back. Ali was not on the group text.

HIS TRUCK WAS FIRST. HE DIDN'T STOP.

"Here," Raiden said as he thrust a T-shirt toward Max, who took it.

The sounds of automatic gunfire came through the pipe, loud enough that Max figured it must be coming from the cab of their truck.

"Raiden, tell me if Zed is texting." Max started tearing the T-shirt into strips. As soon as he had three good-sized strips, he used one as a compress and the other two to secure it against Ezio's head wound.

"You can tie it tighter," Ezio said. "It's not hurting."

He was spewing bullshit, but Max tied it tighter; they needed to get the bleeding under control.

"Zed's not texting," Raiden said.

"Raiden, text Ali and tell him to pull over." Every man had Ali's mobile number.

Screeeccchhhhhh.

Max lurched into Ezio's body, shoving him against the flat steel bars of the cage. Ezio moaned.

We're going to tip over!

Max reached out and found Ezio's head, then curled his arms around it and did his best to roll over so Ezio's body was cuddled against his chest instead of pressed against the bars.

He heard more automatic gunfire, but it was faint. The pipe had likely broken loose, so the sound could be coming from anywhere.

Crrrraaacccccckkkkk.

The impact shuddered through Max. They'd been hit. Zed had to have rammed the side of the truck because they were continuing to move forward.

"Ezio? Raiden? You okay?"

"I'm good. Just looked at my phone. Only text is coming from Cullen wanting to know what's going on." Raiden replied.

"Ezio?" Max asked as he gently shook the man in his arms. He didn't get a reply. "Raiden, how bad was his head injury?"

"His skull wasn't cracked, but a hell of a bump. I'd say he was definitely concussed. What happened to him on the second impact?"

"I fell on top of him and he hit the steel bars. I have no idea if his head hit the steel bars again, but let's just assume they did."

"Max, we can't do anything in the middle of the highway," Raiden solemnly.

He was right, but Max was pretty damn sure that the hijackers had pulled them off onto some side road, and it was the middle of the night.

The truck shuddered to a jolting stop.

"I can't reach my phone—text Raiden and Leo, see what's going on," Max commanded Raiden.

"Already on it." There was a pause. "Have mercy, we have good news." Max heard the grin in Raiden's voice. "This is the text from Leo."

. . .

HIJACKERS ELIMINATED. WILL ASSESS DAMAGE TO TRUCK. MAX, RAIDEN, AND EZIO, HOW ARE YOU?

"Tell Leo the situation. Find out where in the hell we are and see how fast he can get us unloaded."

6

Max got to see the sun come up. They were currently parked in the middle of nowhere; God knew how the truck that Leo was in charge of had managed to limp along, but it had. Max had found it funny that the trucks were actually twenty-two-wheelers in Pakistan, but now he was thankful because the extra tires meant they'd been able to continue to drive to safety.

He pulled the corpse of one of the hijackers out of the cab and let it fall to the ground with a thud, then grimaced with pain. He dragged it the forty meters over to where the other corpse was that Leo had disposed of, then ripped off the man's bloody overshirt. He took off his less bloodstained undershirt and carried it with him as he walked back to Leo's truck.

Max leaned against the seat, contemplating wiping up the gross amount of blood with the dead man's shirt. He was amazed that there wasn't a scratch on Leo.

"Take off your gear," Kane said emphatically as he walked toward him.

"I'm fine," Max assured him.

"That's not going to fly. Raiden told me you were injured and he's worried about your lung. Take off your gear and let me check you out."

"I'm fine." Max started to heft himself up into the truck, then took a step back.

Dammit.

Kane looked him in the eye. "Don't fuck around. I'm serious, take off your gear."

Max stood up and started pulling off his body armor. "Have we received any transmissions from the commander?" he asked.

"Nothing from the States. I haven't sent anything, figured I'd wait until we got to Kandahar. Checked in with Ali, he's bringing the third truck here. We really want all the trucks to arrive in Kandahar at the same time."

Max hissed in a breath as he pulled his shirt over his head.

"Jesus, you really did a number on yourself." Kane winced. The bruise was on his back, so Max couldn't get a good look at it or probe it himself to see if it was a real problem. "This looks like a perfect bullseye," Kane said right before he started palpitations. Max gritted his teeth as he waited to hear his friend's conclusions.

"I'm not feeling that any of your bones are loose, and this happened over ninety minutes ago, so I'd say your lung is fine. But you definitely have one or two cracked ribs. I'm going and getting Raiden's pack and getting some pain meds. Take them if you need them. I'm serious, Max. I'm also going to grab a compression bandage and tape you up. You're going to need that with all the gear in these goddamn cages and for whatever else comes our way, but they'll come off at night so you breathe deeply. That will ward off pneumonia."

"Whatever." As long as his lung wasn't compromised, he knew the drill—six weeks before he'd be back to normal.

Zed walked up to him, wiping the sweat off his forehead with a towel. Max looked over at the truck Leo had been driving and saw that all of the tires had been replaced, but it still wasn't straight.

"Can you break it down for me? I want to know exactly what happened." Max had been too busy helping Raiden with Ezio to get the details earlier.

"The hijackers pulled out in a van in front of Leo, causing him to swerve off A75. I don't know what happened to the driver of the van, he took off, but one had an AK47 and pulled it on Leo and that's when he and his buddy boarded the truck. Meanwhile, I pulled over to the side of the road about a quarter of a mile back. When I did, I grabbed my MP7 from under the seat and texted everyone. Thank God they needed Leo to drive the truck so they didn't kill him. When they started back up, I followed."

Max nodded and Kane came back with the compression bandage and started to apply it.

"And then?" Max asked.

"They pulled off the highway. I followed, figured I would get in front of them and stop them, or shove them to the side of the road. Anything." Zed shrugged.

Max understood. It was a crapshoot; Zed had to do something and he was flying blind.

"As soon as I started pulling up to their side, they started shooting. I sideswiped them and Leo took advantage and took one of them out. But the shooting kept happening, so I knew it wasn't over with so I plowed into the rear—not too hard, didn't want to kill you guys," Zed grinned.

"Much appreciated," Max gave a wan grin.

"Did you consider us?" Kane gave Zed an exasperated look.

"Not really." Zed shrugged his shoulders.

"Max, by the time your truck pulled over to the road and I got to the cab, it looked like a slaughterhouse. I don't know how he got that truck to a stop and wrestled the gun away and kill him, but he did." Now Zed was grinning.

"Yeah, fat lot of good you were," Leo said as he wandered up. "You kept ramming the truck and messing with my aim."

Max looked at the two men; they didn't look any worse for the wear. He glanced over to where Raiden was kneeling beside the back of Zed's truck. Ezio was lying down underneath it for some shade.

"Are you done doctoring me?" Max asked Kane. "I want to check on Ezio."

"The bleeding has stopped, and he's conscious," Kane said as he picked up Max's shirt and helped him put it back on.

"Is he going to be all right making it to Kandahar?" Leo asked.

"As long as there aren't any more hijackers," Kane said.

"Is he going to need to rest when we get there? Should we suss out a friendly that he can stay with while we go find Ms. Sorensen?" Zed asked.

"Raiden will assess Ezio's situation when we arrive. In the meantime, we got some intel from the States. Ms. Sorensen called her mother; she's in Towri. Her mother said to save her cell phone charge and turn it on at midnight, oh-six-hundred, noon, eighteen-hundred, then midnight again, leave it on for half-hour intervals."

"Smart woman," Max said.

They all looked up as they heard Ali's truck lumbering toward them. Good—Leo and Zed could use another pair of hands to pack up the plaster bags. They needed to get a move on to Towri.

MAX FINALLY BREATHED a sigh of relief when he saw Cullen, Asher, and Kostya show up on the second floor of the bombed-out building here in Towri. It was oh-three-hundred on Friday morning, and the trucks were parked miles apart from one another. Leo, Zed, and Ali were all staying with the trucks. There was no other choice, the plaster would be stolen otherwise.

Kostya strode up to Max. "What's the plan?" he asked. The man was having a hard time keeping himself from growling. Kostya didn't like not being in charge.

"Everybody, just huddle up. We've scrounged some food and water, let's eat and I'll fill you in."

Kostya glanced down at the food lying on the plastic bags then picked up three of the figs and a handful of nuts.

Max waited until everybody had helped themselves to food before he explained what he knew so far.

"I talked to Lark Sorensen at midnight. She is going to have her phone on again at oh-six-hundred hours. But what she told me at midnight was that she is currently sheltered with Samira Nuri and her two small girls in a basement apartment in the center of the town. The apartment is owned by a member of the Taliban who died in the street fighting. She saw him die, but because he was shot in the face, nobody knows he is dead so she feels they are safe in his apartment."

"Makes sense," Kostya said.

"They're out of food. Samira is not in the apartment right now; she's been gone since last night."

"Fuck," Asher groaned.

"Lark missed two calls from her, to call her back. When she did at midnight, she didn't reach Samira. Lark's hoping that the next time her phone is turned on, she and Samira will connect. So here's the plan."

Max looked around the small circle of men.

"I have Samira's number. I've called her, but from now on, Kostya, I think the calls need to come from you since you knew her husband better. Then we're going to go and pull out Lark and the girls. If we're lucky, Samira will have already arrived. Samira and the girls will go with Raiden."

"Nope, they should come with me," Kostya said emphatically.

"Absolutely not, they need to go with Raiden, he's the medic. If something goes wrong, he can handle it." Max glared at Kostya, who finally nodded in agreement.

"Kane, you're going with Ezio, you're another fully trained medic."

"If I have to ride with Kane, so do you, Max," Ezio smirked.

"He's right," Kane said.

Max shrugged. "Then I want Lark, Kostya, Cullen, and Nic riding with Leo. The rest of us will go with Ali. I don't want anyone but the Nuri family and Raiden together; too many in that cage will scare the girls."

Everybody nodded.

"How far are we from the apartment?" Asher asked.

Kane pulled out his bulletproof tablet and pulled up a map. "This is the best we had on Towri before we pulled out and the Taliban took over. Here's where we are." He pointed to a spot. "From what Max told me, I *think* this is where Lark and the Nuris are. It's my best guess."

Max had already been over this five times with Kane.

"I want Asher and Cullen across the street on top of these buildings, or what's left of these buildings." He pointed to what he was talking about. "I don't think we're going to need sniper coverage, but in case we do, you'll be there."

"I want one man for each person in the apartment. That's Kostya, Nic, Raiden, and me. Kane, I want you to stay back and listen in to all the chatter. You're going to coordinate what's going on. Kostya, you'll stay with Lark and go directly to Leo's truck." Max waited and Kostya nodded.

"Raiden, Nic, and I will take the Nuris to Zed's truck. Nic and I will help Zed pack them in. Then Nic and I will head over to Leo's truck and make sure Lark is packed in. Then I'll head over to Ali's truck."

"That doesn't make sense," Kane protested. "You should just straight over to Ali's truck once you're done with the Nuri family."

Max looked around and everyone was nodding. He was reluctant because Lark was who they needed to get out.

"I see your point. Since Leo and Ali switched trucks, and Leo is now driving the decent one, then I'm fine with that suggestion. I'll head to where Ali is driving."

Everyone stood up. They had a plan.

7

THEY WERE OUTSIDE THE APARTMENT BUILDING WHEN MAX heard Kostya's voice come over his receiver. "Samira is calling in on my cell phone."

"Take it and keep coming with us," Max ordered.

Max had a tough time hearing the muffled Arabic as he and Nic went around to the back of the building. The back alley was empty so he pushed the wooden door open and stepped down the crumbling cement steps to a narrow, dark hallway. There were no numbers on the doors. Lark had said that the apartment was the first one on the right when you entered from the front. Max saw one shadow up ahead.

"Kostya, report," he whispered into his mic.

"Samira is coming. I'm waiting outside for Cullen or Asher to catch sight of her."

"Good."

Max got in front of the correct door and knocked twice, paused, then knocked twice again. The door was immediately opened a tiny crack by a woman who was covered in a long dress with a scarf covering her head. Her eyes were squinched tight with strain. She could be any Afghan woman except for her light blue eyes.

"Ms. Sorensen?" Max whispered.

She flung the door wide.

"Get in here, fast and quiet."

Max, Nic, and Kane swarmed into the small space and Max looked around for the girls, but realized they must be behind the drape at the far end of the room.

"Where's Kostya Barona?"

For a moment, Max was startled that Lark knew what Kostya looked like, then realized he was dealing with a Pulitzer Prize-winning journalist; of course, she would have found a way to get Kostya's picture.

"Kostya's waiting for Samira outside. She got ahold of him."

"Good," Lark nodded. "Let me wake up the girls." She waved her arm to the small little kitchen area. "Grab their backpacks."

Max grinned when he saw two Hello Kitty backpacks. It made him happy for just an instant for the little girls. Nic grabbed the backpacks before he could. Nic was grinning too.

Max listened to the sounds of little girls' voices behind the curtain, then Lark was ushering out two tiny girls. One had to be only five at the most. She was ushering them towards a door, telling them they needed to hurry and go to the bathroom.

"I'm hungry," one of the girls wailed petulantly.

"Hush, Nazy," the taller girl said in Arabic. "Mama is getting us food. Use the toilet. We're going on an adventure." Then she stopped still as she took note of Max and the others. When the other girl turned to see what her sister was looking at she let out a shrill shriek.

"Nazy, stop!" the older girl said as she clamped her hand over her mouth.

Lark crouched down in front of them and started whispering softly. The small girl started nodding, then she turned to go to the bathroom. The tall girl continued to stare at them. She didn't move until it was her turn to go to the bathroom.

The littlest girl stood next to Lark and held her leg as she stared at Nic longingly. Nic caught on and moved forward slowly. In halting Arabic he asked her which backpack was hers. She pointed to the one in his left hand and he handed it to her. When her older sister came out of the bathroom, he handed the other backpack to her. She gave him a hesitant smile and thanked him.

"Where's Mama?" the older girl asked.

"She's getting food," Lark said easily.

The door opened and everyone looked up.

Nazy yelled, "Mama!"

"Shhhhhh," Samira said as she caught her running daughter. "You must be quiet." Kostya closed the door behind them. He raised his eyebrow at Max.

"Ms. Sorensen, do you have everything ready to go for you and Mrs. Nuri?"

She darted behind the curtain and came back with one worn Swiss Gear backpack that had to belong to Lark and a bulging, paisley cloth bag.

"We're ready." She opened a side pocket on her backpack and pulled out a pouch. "Inside are the Afghan Special Immigrant Visas that Ebrahem acquired before he died. There is one for Samira and the two girls." Her hand trembled as she handed them to Max.

Max looked at them, then handed them to Raiden.

"He's going to be going to be traveling with Samira and her daughters, he'll keep them."

Lark nodded.

"Okay, we're heading out," Max said. He turned to Samira who was holding Nazy. "Do you think your older daughter will be comfortable going with Lark, while Nazy stays with you?"

"Taja, come here." Samira nodded to the older girl. She knelt down, still holding her youngest daughter in her arms. Taja crossed the small room to her mother. "I need you to be brave and stay with Miss Lark. She and some of the men are going to keep you safe, while Nazy and I will go with the other men."

Taja grabbed her mother around her neck. "I don't want to leave you," she cried. The girl's tears had Max dropping to his knees.

"Listen to me," he whispered to the scared little girl. "By daylight, you, your Mama, and your sister will all be together, I promise you, Taja."

She lifted her head out of the crook of her mother's neck and her big, soulful brown eyes stared at him. "Truly?"

"Yes, truly."

"Are you taking us to our Papa?" she asked.

Max's mouth dried up, and when he tried to answer, no words came out.

"Papa's in heaven," Nazy said.

"Are you taking us to heaven?" Taja asked him.

"*Habeebti*, we're taking you somewhere safe, where you can run and play outside anytime you want. Won't that be fun?" Max asked. "But no, your papa won't be there, I'm sorry."

"Taja, we will talk about your papa again when we are safe, okay?" Samira said to her daughter.

"Yes, Mama."

"Now go to Ms. Lark. You must be brave so that we can get to safety, okay?"

The little girl nodded, then walked into Lark's waiting arms.

Max stood up and backed up two steps. "Asher?" he asked into his mic. "Are we clear?"

"Go out the back. I've seen two jeeps drive by since you've been inside."

"Okay, we're all heading to Zed's truck first since that's where the Nuri family is going. Once they're dropped off, we'll head to Leo's and make sure that Lark is situated.

"Cullen, you're going to take point when Kostya and Nic head out with the baby and her mother." His eyes flicked up at Nic, who nodded. Max had seen Nazy's eyes light up with Nic when he'd passed her the backpack; *that should work.* Nic sidled up to Samira and her daughter as Max continued to give orders.

"Raiden, you take up the rear behind the Samira, Nazy, Kostya, Nic group." Raiden nodded. "I want you guys going first. Make sense?" All of his men nodded. Max handed Raiden Lark's backpack and Samira's cloth bag.

He told Samira, Lark, and the girls the plan. Samira carried Nazy over to Taja and gave her a big hug. Then she stood up and went to the door. Nazy clung to her mother when Nic tried to take her into his arms. It took him a minute, but somehow he got the little girl to giggle, and then she clung to his neck.

"Okay, start moving," Max commanded. Nazy waved to her sister over Nic's shoulder. Samira blew her oldest daughter a kiss.

Max watched as they all headed out the door. Max walked over to Lark and Taja then got down on his knees. "What do you think about me carrying you, *habeebti*?"

Taja gave a shy smile.

"That's good."

He got up and turned to his men. He tapped his mic. "Cullen you're covering us. Kane, you've got Lark, and Ezio you're taking the rear."

"Imagine that," Ezio said dryly as he touched the bandage on his head.

"Fuck that noise," Kane growled at him. "If you screw up while you're watching our backs just because you have a concussion, I'll lay you out on your ass."

Ezio grinned.

"We're going to wait another ten minutes, then we're going."

Ezio picked up the two small bags of food and water that Kostya had dropped by the door. He rummaged around the small apartment to see if there was anything else that might be of use. He came back from behind the drape with a ragged-looking stuffed cat and two blankets that he had rolled up. *Good.* They would help in the Nuri cage. So would the ChemLights.

"I DON'T LIKE THIS," Lark said as she looked at Kostya and Max. It was the fifty-third time she had raised an objection. *It must be a reporter thing.* Max looked over at Raiden sitting cross-legged inside the cage with Taja on his lap and his iPhone playing music softly next to her ear. Any man who had a mophi had also given theirs up for the cause, anything to keep the kids occupied during the journey. Nazy was sleeping in her mother's lap with the stuffed cat in her arms.

"Lark, shut up and be reasonable." Kostya glowered at her.

Max saw what apparently Kostya didn't; Lark was scared for the girls and Samira, and she was hiding it under a layer of bitchy.

"Ms. Sorensen, it's going to be alright, this will work," Max said trying to reassure her.

She swung her head to glare at him. "How? It's over seven hundred kilometers to the Torkham border crossing. I looked it up—the Chaman border crossing is only two-hundred and fifty kilometers, why aren't we crossing there?"

"Two reasons. We used that crossing to get into Afghanistan two days ago and they'll recognize us coming back with the same payload. Second, we need to get to Islamabad. That will be the easier airport to get the Nuri family out of Pakistan. Torkham is a lot closer to Islamabad than Chaman."

Max watched her tortured expression as the bags were piled higher on the truck and the faces of the girls were covered up.

"Lark, you've got to trust us. This is our job, this is what we're trained to do," Kostya said in a soft voice.

Lark turned to Kostya and Max could see that his words had gotten through. "I just wish I could be with them."

Kostya ran his hand down her arm. "I know you do, but Raiden is our medic; he needs to be the one with them. You know that's the best choice, and those cages are too small for one more person."

She bowed her head and nodded. Max noted that

when Kostya's hand landed next to hers, she grabbed it and tangled her fingers with his. If that would help her get through the next day, then he was all for it.

His phone vibrated. The text was from Zed; he'd needed to stretch his legs, so he'd sent him out to hunt and gather. His ETA was five minutes. They'd given most of their food and water supplies to Raiden and the Nuris, knowing that they would have an opportunity to get more.

Asher and Kane jumped off the top of the truck. "We can move out when Zed gets back," Asher said.

It still was an hour before dawn; they needed to get Lark loaded as soon as possible.

"Ezio, Cullen, and Ms. Sorensen, you get into the cab with Zed. He'll drive you to the next truck that Leo's driving. We'll follow on foot." He didn't need to tell Cullen what his job was. He got in last so that Ezio and Lark were placed in the middle. Cullen was literally riding shotgun in case there was trouble.

Max, Kane Asher, Nic, and Kostya started hauling ass. It was four kilometers to the next truck, but they needed to stay out of sight. It took them more than a minute, and Max was more than a little pissed to see that Kostya was already at the truck pulling off bags of plaster without looking winded by the time he got there.

"You're injured," Kane said quietly when he saw Max's face.

"Why'd you say that?"

"Cause your nose is out of joint that Kostya beat you so bad," Kane smirked. "Now get to work."

My friend is an asshole.

By the time they were done getting Kostya, Cullen, Lark, and Nic loaded onto the second truck, the sun had risen. Asher, Max, Kane, and Ezio all hitched rides in Leo and Zed's trucks to the third truck that Ali had driven. When they got there, they found that Ali had already unpacked the bags so that the cage was unveiled.

"Hurry," Ali said. He was definitely hyped up.

Max and his men got into the cage and they watched as Ali, Zed, and Leo loaded the bags of plaster and closed them inside. Max said a quick prayer that this would work.

8

Max waited for the text to tell them what checkpoint they were at. He prayed it was Torkham. Ezio was sleeping too damn much and he was worried. The good news was that Raiden said that the girls were physically fine and had no meltdowns. The truck continued to move forward in spits and starts.

AT TORKHAM. CAN'T SEE CHECKPOINT. LINE COULD BE JUST A MILE, OR MANY MILES.

That text was from Leo.

Max and his team were down to their last two liters of water. They needed to get out of this cage.

They moved forward again, then stopped. It continued like that for hours, and Max found himself going in and out of sleep.

When the stopping and starting finally changed into a long stop, Max sat up straight.

. . .

THEY'RE PUSHING SWORDS INTO THE BAGS.

The text was from Zed. He was the lead truck.

Jesus, don't let either of the girls be hurt.

Max thought past that initial reaction, then calmed down. A sword wouldn't get past two layers of bags. They were good. But would they notice where the bags weren't packed so closely together to allow air to come in?

"Fuck," Kane hissed. "This is taking forever."

It was. Max had been staring at his watch. This was the longest time they'd been stopped since they'd gotten to the Torkham checkpoint. As the second hand passed twelve again he thought his brain would explode.

Eight minutes.

Max and the three others with him all let out sighs of relief when their truck started moving forward. They didn't move far before they were stopped again. It was Leo's turn. Max started looking at his watch.

Six minutes.

Max didn't use the plastic pipe to listen; he and the others just sat tight. He grinned in relief when the truck started moving after four minutes.

Roger, Nigel, and Randall were going to meet them outside of Peshawar. It was just another fifty miles. The men were supposed to have figured out places for them to stay.

Leo texted again.

EVERYONE IS IN PAKISTAN

. . .

Max pulled up his text to Roger and let him know where they were and gave an update on the situation with Ezio. He wanted specific coordinates on where they should take the trucks. He didn't have to wait long for a response. They would be pulling up to a farm five miles outside of Peshawar where the trucks could be unloaded. Roger had arranged for the family to go on vacation for a week. Max had no idea how, but he was impressed.

Roger went on to text that everyone would be staying at the farm for at least one night before getting into the vehicles he and the Brits had arranged to get them to Islamabad. They would be taking multiple flights out to Dubai and the airport in Doha, Qatar. Since the Nuri family had their Afghan Special Immigrant Visas, they would be allowed to fly out.

Max relaxed against the bars. There was a plan!

By the time they stopped in Peshawar, Ezio was unconscious again, so Roger and the Brits as well as the three drivers needed to work to unpack the truck he was in first. Max had let Roger know the situation, so the former Army Ranger would be working his contacts to find medical care, and if necessary he would be figuring out how to get Ezio to a good hospital.

"His breathing is still shallow but his pulse is good," Kane reported to no one in particular.

Max and Asher had shoved aside four bags as soon as they passed over into Pakistan so that a good amount of air was getting into the cage for Ezio to breathe. The

ChemLight that they had activated didn't give them a good idea of whether his color was looking healthy or pale.

"Do you think it's a brain bleed?" Max asked again.

Kane shot him a frustrated look.

"Sorry, man." Max knew better. There wasn't any way for Kane to really know that, but considering the fact that Ezio had been unconscious for the last two hours, he needed a CT scan, that was for damn sure.

ARRIVED

IT WAS A TEXT FROM ZED. Their truck came to an abrupt halt. Max heard the sounds of people above them. They had to be unhitching the belts holding in the bags of plaster. At this point they didn't have to be careful with the bags anymore, they could just toss them on the ground and let them split open—anything to get Ezio out of this damn cage.

Minutes that seemed like hours passed, and Max sighed with relief when he saw the gray polluted sky overhead.

"Hey there. Good to see you." Roger looked down at them. "How's our boy Stark?" he asked, referring to Ezio.

"Quit with the pleasantries and get us the hell out of here," Kane growled. Max watched as Kane lifted Ezio's eyelids so he could check out his pupils.

"We've got a little triage area set up in the house," Roger said.

"I said—" Kane started.

"They're hurrying," Max said as he watched the bags

in front of the side panel of the cage rapidly falling off the truck.

"Move back," Zed cautioned as he opened the cage door. Leo and Zed held out their arms to take Ezio off the truck. Kane jumped off after them. "Where to?" he asked Roger.

"Follow me." Roger started jogging past a row of boxes that Max thought might be honey bee hives, but he wasn't sure.

When Kane went to carry Ezio in his arms, Zed shook his head. "I've got him. I haven't been stuck in a cage for twenty hours."

"You're right, but I'm going with you." Kane glowered.

"Wouldn't have expected anything less," Zed agreed.

Max watched them all head for a house a little ways in the distance, with a narrow drive that the trucks would not have passed through. He turned his attention to Zed's truck because he wanted to get the little girls out of the cramped cage as soon as possible. Leo, Ali, the two Brits, and Asher were already working on it.

Max started pulling down sacks of plaster from the right side of the flatbed and smiled when he heard the little girls' excited laughter.

"Mama, look. I can see sky!" one of the little Nuri girls said.

"Shhhhh, Nazy," Samira cautioned.

"It's all right, Samira," Raiden said. "We're safe now."

When the last bag was pulled away and the four occupants of the cage were uncovered, Max couldn't help but be impressed by Raiden Sato. There his man was, looking calm and relaxed as he held Taja in his lap as he introduced her to Leo.

"And there's the house where we are going to be

spending the night." He pointed at the house in the distance.

"Will there be a potty inside?" Nazy asked her mom.

"Yes, *habeebti*," Max said as he opened up the door of the cage. "There will be a potty, and a bed for you. Won't that be nice?"

She hugged her bedraggled stuffed cat close, looked at him beneath her long lashes, and nodded. She then turned her head and looked up at her mother. "Who's that?"

"He's one of the nice men who are helping us," she answered.

"I'm Max," he said as he held out his hands to her. "I like your cat," he said in Arabic. "What's his name?"

"*Her* name is Kitty," she said.

"Will you let me help you and Miss Kitty out of the truck?" Max asked.

She looked back up at her mother, who nodded, then she crawled over to Max and let him lift her out of the cage and onto the ground.

"Mrs. Nuri, can I help you out?" Max asked. Samira nodded, and he helped her out of the truck. He turned again to Taja. "And how about you, beautiful Taja, can I help you down?" Max asked. She grinned at him and giggled.

"Yes please."

Raiden winked at him as he lifted Taja and placed her into Max's waiting arms. She didn't let go of Max; instead, she held onto his neck. "Is there really a bed in the house?" she asked.

"Yes," he answered, hoping he wasn't telling a lie. "But I've got to put you down now because I have to help Ms. Lark out of her truck, okay?"

Taja nodded shyly. "Okay."

Max turned and saw that the other truck was damn near unpacked. He started on over there to check on all of the passengers.

"I'm fine," he heard Lark Sorensen say loudly. "I can get out on my own."

"You've been cramped in here forever, Lark. Let Zed help you. Have you ever heard the phrase cutting off your nose to spite your face?" Kostya growled.

Sounds like those two are getting along just great. Max looked over and saw Cullen was fighting not to laugh. Nic was looking like he was watching a tennis match.

When Lark tried to get down off the truck on her own steam she almost fell on her butt, but Zed caught her in his arms before she could. He saw Lark's face turn red with embarrassment.

"You just couldn't wait for some help, could you, you stubborn woman?" Kostya sighed as he shook his head.

"Maybe I just wanted this big guy to catch me, did you ever think of that, Barona?"

"Hey, Max, Nic and I have a bet going on. Ten to one says that Lark and Kostya will be sleeping together in less than a month. Five to one, it will be three months. Even money, six months. Want in on the action?" Cullen yelled over at Max.

"I'll take the ten to one odds," Leo yelled out.

Lark started struggling to get out of Zed's arms as he yelled out that he would take even money. "Ms. Sorensen, calm down," Zed tried to soothe her. "The fact that I'm taking even money means that I believe you'll give the lieutenant a run for his money."

Lark kept kicking until Zed had no choice but to put her down. "My next exposé is going to be a comparison of the maturity level between boys' high school athletes and America's Special Forces. *My* bet is that the high school boys will end up looking more mature." Lark smiled sweetly.

Cullen hooted with laughter.

Lark sauntered over to Samira and the girls. He watched as they all started walking to the house with Raiden carrying one of the girls in each arm.

ROGER HAD DONE a great job of getting vehicles for everyone to travel to Islamabad. Since Ezio had been conscious for the last thirty-two hours, he, Raiden, and Asher went first, they were booked on a direct flight from Islamabad to Germany where Ezio would be checked out at the US Landstuhl Army Medical Center.

Next would be the Nuri family. Lark had been making calls to the United States ever since she'd stopped bickering with Kostya. Max had overheard her talking to her mother and he was sure that the Nuri family was going to find a soft landing when they reached America. Lark was going to be on the flight that would take them home.

"I'm going with them," Kostya said when Kane started to arrange the flights.

"Do you think that is really such a good idea?" Kane asked reasonably. "You and Ms. Sorensen get along as well as the Joker and Batman."

"It makes sense. We made up that extensive paper trail; it would look odd if I didn't go with her."

"He's right," Max said as he looked over Kane's shoulder at the kitchen table. Kane shrugged. "But send

Nic with them. He's doing really well with Nazy so that should help on the international flights."

"I've got the van waiting," Roger said as he walked into the kitchen. "Have you figured everything out yet?"

"Yes," Kane said without looking up from the tablet. "Kostya, start rounding up your charges and try not to piss off Ms. Sorensen in the process."

Kostya glowered at Kane's lowered head and Max grinned as he left the room.

"Kane, that just leaves you, me, Cullen, Leo, and Zed. Book us through either Qatar or UAE and get us back to Crete, then we'll pick up our gear and take a military transport home."

Kane looked up at Max. "Already done."

"Of course it is, what in the hell was I thinking?" Max sat down in the seat beside him. "Do we have time to send a report to the commander?"

Kane gave him a broad grin. "Of course I arranged for enough time."

Max laughed, and they got to work.

9

Max landed in Virginia at damn near midnight, with Zed, Leo, Kane, and Cullen. He'd had good news all around on the last leg of his journey. Ezio's CT scan came back showing fluid around the brain which had caused all of his symptoms, but even in the twenty-four hours he'd been at the hospital in Germany the fluid had decreased. Raiden and Asher were on their way home.

Meanwhile, Nic had told him that Kostya and Lark had played nice the entire trip to California and that Lark's mother, Beatrice Allen, had been at the airport to greet her daughter. She'd come with her own security team and a nanny to help with the Nuri girls. Beatrice had whisked her daughter and the Nuris into a limo before the bags were even claimed, so Kostya and Nic should be back soon.

With all the information that he received, he was fine to talk to Commander Clark who was waiting for him at the airport. Max nodded to Asher, Zed, and Leo as they broke off to head home and Kane stayed with him to go with the commander into his office. As soon as Simon's door was shut and he was seated behind his desk he asked, "Why was Kostya Barona really with you?"

Max thought rapidly. "Kane, I know A.J. is waiting for you, you're dismissed."

Kane didn't look happy, but he left the room and shut the door after himself.

Simon ran his fingers through his salt-and-pepper hair. "Shit, this isn't good if you had to let Kane go. Are you going to try to take this all onto your shoulders?"

"It was my mission, so it's my decision. I had information that turned out to be right, that Ms. Sorensen would not leave Afghanistan without Samira Nuri and her two daughters. She had been in contact with Kostya so I knew there was some trust there, and I also knew that there was trust between Kostya and Samira because he had worked so closely with her dead husband. It was my determination his help would be critical."

Simon stared at him for one of the longest minutes of his life.

"Is that the story you're sticking with?"

"It's the truth." There was no reason to get into how they had created a back-dated cover story. Max refused to lie to his commander and Simon knew it, which was why he didn't ask any follow-up questions.

"Good job on completing your mission," Simon smiled wryly. "Now get out of here and get some sleep. Tell the rest of your team, including Barona, that when they touch down, they don't have to report in to me."

Max's smile was relieved and grateful. "I will. Thank you."

"Get out of here."

THE KNOCKING on his door would not stop. Max pulled the third pillow over his ears to try to drown it out. When it finally stopped he breathed a sigh of relief. But the peace didn't last long, as he soon heard tapping on his bedroom window.

"Max? Are you home now? I saw your truck."

"I'm not home, Mikey," Max yelled out.

Mikey laughed. "Yes, you are. Dad said not to bother you, but we're going to get ice cream later, did you want to go?"

"I'll go tomorrow."

"We might not go tomorrow."

Max pushed his naked body upright and got out of bed. He walked over to his dresser and pulled on a pair of sweat pants then opened the blinds. He blinked at the bright sunlight as he opened the window so that he was better able to talk to Mikey.

"I promise to take you to get ice cream tomorrow, okay, buddy? But I've got other stuff I need to do today."

Like calling a lawyer who was probably a centenarian.

"Okay, I'll come back tomorrow," Michael said with a huge smile.

Max headed to his kitchen and started the coffee. Even though he had showered last night, he still wanted another one. Sometimes it took three or four showers after a mission before he really felt clean again. This time, after all those hours in the cage, he might need a bath!

He went back to his bedroom where his phone was charging and checked all of the messages that he'd avoided while he'd been out of the country. Just how many people in the world sold insurance, anyway? And, how in the hell did he get on their calling lists?

He read the message from Gray Tyler, the lieutenant of the Black Dawn SEAL team out of Coronado, California. His wife would be lecturing in D.C. next month and he wanted to go out to dinner. Max sent a quick text back accepting the invitation, then went and got in the shower. By the time he was done the coffee was ready and he could face the day. First order of business? Call Elias Peterson. His letter was propped up against the empty fruit bowl on his kitchen table. By the tenth ring he was getting pretty damned frustrated—why in the hell wasn't it going to voicemail?

"Peterson," a loud cranky voice answered.

Hell, was he talking to a former Marine drill sergeant?

"My name is Max Hogan. I'm calling to speak with Elias Peterson."

He heard the man take a deep breath. "You've got him. What took you so long to respond to my letter?"

"I've been out of the country," Max started to explain.

"This is urgent. I had to hire an investigator, and they're not cheap and it took over a month to find you. So now it's a month and ten days. I need you in my office. We've pussy-footed around enough. I'll see you in an hour."

Max choked down a laugh.

Who was this cranky old man?

Then he sobered up as he remembered he was dealing with Meggie's death.

"I live in Virginia."

"Catch a plane. Be in my office by three o'clock," he said firmly.

"Mr. Peterson, I'm so sorry to hear that Meghan died.

But I don't understand what any of this has to do with me. I only knew her for a short time and that was over five years ago."

"You're one of the beneficiaries in her will. I'm not able to go into details with you at this time, just come to my office."

"Mr. Peterson, I can make it tomorrow, not today," Max said reasonably.

"Today. You're on East Coast time, here in Chicago it is central time. It's eight in the morning where you are, you can make it. Call me when you get to O'Hare."

He hung up.

Max shook his head and stretched. He debated how he felt about the old man's orders, then he decided the old guy was a character. What's more, this will thing had been bugging the shit out of him so he would definitely catch the soonest flight he could to Chicago.

It took Max a minute to find the right office in the old building. It was down the hall and around a corner. He didn't know what to expect, but it sure wasn't the dark wood paneling, the deep green carpeting, and the Persian rug set underneath an antique writing desk. Sitting at the desk was a woman with bright red hair who couldn't be a day younger than sixty.

"Are you Mr. Hogan?" she asked.

"I am," Max confirmed.

"My father was expecting you a half-hour ago," she said. She waved her hand toward the inner door. "Show yourself in."

Father? Just how old is Elias Peterson?

"Thank you," Max smiled. He opened the door and found another beautifully appointed office where two people waited, a man behind a desk and a woman in a chair before it. The huge hand-carved desk dominated the office and made the old man sitting behind it look small.

Until he opened his mouth.

"Hogan, about time you got here." His bushy, gray eyebrows dipped down over his eyes as he glared at Max.

"Mr. Peterson, I called you from the airport and said I was coming."

"That was over two hours ago. Never mind. Sit down." He jabbed his finger at the empty chair in front of him.

"Hello," Max said politely to the woman who sat in the chair next to his. She was dressed in a soft cashmere sweater, pearls, a pencil skirt, and low black heels. Her brown hair was held up in a tight bun. Her jaw was tight too, as were her hands clutching the purse in her lap. When she looked up to respond to his 'hello,' Max could swear he saw fear in her eyes.

What the hell?

"Hello," she whispered.

"Now that you're both here, I can get started. You two are the only adults named in Meghan Todd's will. First, I want to explain that I wrote Meghan's grandmother's will forty years ago. It was airtight. She left her house and money to Meghan, didn't want any of it to go to her no-good son, but that young feller has been causing problems about it ever since Meghan inherited it. That's why when Meghan got the cancer and she knew her time was limited, she wanted me to make up another airtight will, and I have. I'm not going to read the whole damn thing, it's a waste of your time and my time. I've had Pearl make copies for both of you, so I'll summarize it now."

With his gnarled knuckles, he shoved two white envelopes across the desk to each of them. Max grabbed his and pulled out the sheaf of papers.

"Are you hard of hearing Mr. Hogan? What part of, 'I'll summarize it' did you not understand?"

Max looked over at the woman sitting next to him. She hadn't reacted to Elias' comment. What was her deal, why was she so anxious? Max stuffed the papers back into the envelope and slid them down into the side of the seat cushion.

"I'm all ears," he said. He really was. The more the man had built up the situation, the more concerned Max had gotten, and the high level of stress the woman next to him was radiating didn't help.

"Max, five years ago you impregnated Meghan Lancaster when she was on vacation in Tennessee, and she gave birth to a baby boy that she named Zephyr Maxwell Lancaster."

What did he say?

I couldn't have heard right.

The man kept speaking. Words were coming out of his mouth, but they made no sense to Max.

I have a son?

Meghan's face flittered across his mind. She was smiling at the front of the church in her bridesmaid's dress.

She gave birth to my son, and never told me?

"Mr. Hogan?"

I have a little boy?

Max's lungs seized. Fury, shock, and joy were fighting for life under his skin.

"Mr. Hogan," the attorney snapped at him.

"Huh?"

"Did you hear a word I said?" Elias asked.

"I have a son," Max said gruffly.

"Yes, yes, yes. But after that. Did you hear me?"

Max slowly shook his head. He tried hard to focus, but it was as if all the air in the office had vanished. He couldn't breathe.

"I said that when Meghan knew her cancer was terminal she wrote up her will and made you Zephyr's legal guardian. As soon as the DNA test is completed you can petition the court to be instated as his legal father. Meghan has also left her house, 401k, and savings to Zephyr, but unfortunately due to the criminally high level of medical costs in our country these days, most of those assets have been depleted."

"Cancer?"

"Yes. Breast cancer." Elias answered. "He shook his head. "Such a shame."

"How long was she sick?" Max asked quietly.

"Almost a year and a half," the woman spoke up for the first time. Max's entire attention turned to her.

"Who are you?"

"I'm Meghan's best friend. I mean I was. My name is Hannah Woods." Her lower lip trembled. "I've been living with and taking care of Meghan and Zephyr for the last year." Her big green eyes were filled with tears.

"Where's Zephyr now?" Max demanded to know.

"My mom is babysitting him."

Max stood up straight and glared down at her. "I want to see him," he demanded.

"Sit down, young man, we're not done." Max turned to look at Elias, ready to do battle.

"We have things to iron out before you can run off

half-cocked. You're a military man, you understand that certain protocols are necessary."

Max *did* understand. He considered the man's words.

"You need more information. Sit down."

He sat down.

Elias shoved his glasses up his nose and looked down at the papers in front of him. "As I was saying, most of Meghan's assets, including most of the equity in her home, has been depleted paying her medical costs, but not all. As Zephyr's legal and financial guardian, you're going to have to sort that out."

Dazed, Max nodded.

"However, Meghan was a smart girl, and she took out a million-dollar life insurance policy when Zephyr was born and named him the beneficiary. This cannot be touched by the medical bills. Again, as his guardian, Mr. Hogan, you will be responsible for administering all of Zephyr's assets."

Max nodded.

"Hannah, even though you were not named as a beneficiary in the will, Meghan wrote this letter for you." Elias nudged a smaller envelope to her. "She and I talked a long time about how deeply you love Zephyr and she spent a lot of time wavering over whether she should appoint you as Zephyr's legal guardian."

Max's body locked up at the thought of this woman cutting him out of his son's life.

Elias continued. "But Meghan knew that you had felt strongly that Zephyr needed to know his father. One of the final things she told me is that she hopes that you and Maxwell here, will be able to work together to transition things for Zephyr."

Max watched as Hannah leaned forward and picked up the envelope.

"Is there anything else?" Max bit out the question.

"No, that is the end. I will work with you to get the paperwork done to petition the courts to legally instate you as Zephyr's legal father."

"I appreciate that, Mr. Peterson," Max said as he stood up. "But my first order of business is to meet my son."

10

Hannah stood up, shoving the letter into her purse, and doing her best to ignore the man who was a carbon copy of the little boy who she loved with all of her heart. She fumbled with the bigger envelope, trying to push that into her purse as well as Max Hogan held the door open for her. She kept her eyes on the carpet as she stepped by him.

I knew this could happen.
I knew this could happen.

Her purse dropped from her frozen fingers and a large masculine hand was there, handing it back to her. Helplessly, she looked up into determined gray eyes.

"Hannah—" he started.

She whirled away from him and turned to the red-haired secretary. "Where's the ladies' room?"

"They're next to the elevators, you can't miss them," she said without looking up from the tabloid magazine she was reading.

"Hannah, we need to talk," Max said to her as he followed her out into the hall.

Hanna nodded. "I know," she mumbled. "Just give me a minute, okay? I'll meet you in front of the elevators, then we can talk in the lobby."

Max gave her a stiff nod.

As soon as she got to the safety of the bathroom, she went to the sink and ran cold water over her wrists, while avoiding looking at herself in the mirror.

I can't do this. There's no possible way I can do this. She looked up at the water-stained ceiling, trying to stop tears from falling.

I can't lose him.

She'd just finally got him smiling again as she let him make home runs after buying him the T-ball set.

He smiled!

He laughed!

Zephyr'd giggled!

She threw back her head and silently screamed out Zephyr's name.

I can't let him go. I can't!

Pain screamed through her hands and up her arms then burst through her soul.

"Hannah?"

She spun around at Max's voice and saw him at the entryway of the woman's restroom.

"Are you all right? I heard you cry out."

"You look just like him," she whispered.

Is he even real?

She looked down and saw that water had filled up the clogged sink and was now pouring onto the floor. She struggled to turn off the faucets when Max was suddenly there to help her. She saw blood in the water, and that was when she realized she'd dug her fingers so deeply into the porcelain of the sink that she had broken off a couple of her fingernails.

"Come on, let's get you out of here." She watched numbly as Max bent down and picked up her purse sitting in a puddle of water. He held it away from himself as he put his arm around her waist and ushered her out the door toward the elevators.

"How'd you get here today?" he asked.

"Drove."

"I took a cab," Max said. "Why don't we go together to wherever Zephyr is, okay?"

She nodded. It was like her brain was somewhere outside of her body. She was still trying to soak it all in. She knew. Ever since Elias had told her he was trying to track down another person for the reading of the will, she *knew* this was probably going to happen, but how was she going to survive?

They went outside. Even the weak Chicago sunlight hurt her eyes.

"Where are you parked?" Max asked.

Hannah had to think for a minute. "Up the block," she answered.

He held onto her elbow as they walked down the crowded street to the paid parking lot. She pointed to her Honda.

"Are you okay to drive?" Max asked.

She considered his question. Had anyone ever asked that before?

"Are you offering to drive?" she asked.

"Yeah. It looks like you could use a break." His smile was compassionate.

How come he's not the one in shock? Oh yeah, he won. He got Zephyr.

"Do you know your way around Chicago?" she asked.

"I'll manage. Give me the keys."

She handed them to him, then he surprised her by opening the passenger door for her. She got in and rested her head against the headrest. She was so tired.

They made it to her mother's little house in Buffalo Grove where Hannah had grown up. She directed Max to park in the driveway, and just let herself in the front door.

"Why isn't it locked?" Max demanded to know.

"I don't know, it never is," Hannah said. She yelled up the stairs. "Mom, I'm home. I've got a visitor."

Her mother rushed down the stairs in her pink capri pants and yellow sweater. "Don't yell, Zephyr is taking his nap," she admonished her daughter, then she stopped dead.

"So this is him?"

Hannah slumped. "Yes."

She took the final two steps down the stairs and took Hannah into her arms. She looked over her daughter's shoulder and whimpered. "Zephyr is his spitting image."

Hannah nodded, then turned around and gave Max a weak smile.

"Max Hogan, this is my mother, Julie Woods."

She stepped around her daughter, keeping her arm around her waist. "It's nice to meet you." Trust her mother to keep up the Midwestern politeness no matter what the situation, but then she looked up at Hannah. "Are you okay, Honey?"

"I'll get there," Hannah said as she gave her mother a wan smile.

"We had an idea of how the reading of the will would go," her mother admitted as she gestured toward the kitchen. "Would you like something to eat or drink while we wait for Zephyr to wake up from his nap?"

"When will that be?" Max asked anxiously, not making a move.

Julie looked confused as she turned to her daughter.

"Mom, when did you put Zeph down?"

"He went to sleep maybe ten minutes ago," she answered.

Hannah turned to Max. "He usually sleeps for at least an hour. Let's talk in the kitchen over something to drink, okay?" She knew she sounded pitiful, but she needed something to do, she needed a respite.

Max looked up the stairs, then turned and smiled at Hannah and her mom. "Okay," he said as he followed the two women into the spacious kitchen that was filled with top-of-the-line stainless steel appliances.

"Max, what would you like to drink? We have all kinds of juices, and my husband keeps the refrigerator filled with a plethora of different types of beers," Julie said as she motioned to the kitchen table.

"Water's fine."

"Sparkling or plain?" Julie asked.

"Plain water is fine by me."

Hannah watched Max's expression as her mother pulled out a pitcher filled with ice and limes to pour him a glass of water. Most of her friends looked startled, but Max seemed to take it in stride.

"Lemonade, Honey?" she asked Hannah.

"Yes, please. How was Zephyr today?" she asked her mom as Julie sat down at the table with two glasses of lemonade.

"All he could talk about was the t-ball set that you'd

gotten him. Apparently, he only makes home runs; is that true?" Julie asked slyly.

"He hits the ball pretty far off the tee, and he loves to run the bases, so I can't bear to tag him out," Hannah admitted. She was tracing patterns on her glass in the condensation. She tried to think of something else to say, but she couldn't.

Julie reached out and touched Max's hand resting on the table. "You'll never know how relieved my daughter and I are to know that Zephyr will get a chance to grow up knowing his father. I've prayed for this day. I just wish to God it could have been under happier circumstances."

"If you were Meggie's best friend, can you tell me why in God's name she never reached out to me to tell me that I'd gotten her pregnant?" Hannah's head jerked up as those first raw words were ripped out of his throat.

Christ, just how much pain would all of them have to endure?

"Or for that matter," Max continued. "Can you tell me what I could have possibly done wrong that made her ghost me after our time in Tennessee?"

Hannah took a deep breath. She hated this.

"Mr. Hogan, you have to understand, Meghan's life wasn't easy. She had her demons." Max pulled his arm out from underneath her mother's hand.

"What do you mean by that?" Max frowned.

"I mean that she was fragile. Her life was hard, and it was important to be understanding," Julie Woods tried to explain.

"Mom, let me answer his questions," Hannah shook her head. "I know you loved Meghan like another daughter, but sometimes you made too many excuses."

Hannah felt bobby pins drop to the floor as she ran her fingers through her hair in distress.

"You can't speak ill of the dead," her mother said firmly.

Hannah stood up. "Max, would you like to take a walk?"

Max stood up and nodded.

Hannah ignored her mother's hurt look. They'd never agreed on this, but they always loved one another, and that was the important thing.

Max held the front door open for them. "Julie, lock up behind us, will you?"

"That's not necessary, Max," she called out.

"Humor me."

For the first time today, Hannah felt her mouth twitch as she saw her mother come to the door to lock up behind them as they walked down the front porch steps. As soon as they got to the bottom, Max gently grabbed her elbow to stop her.

"Do you want to go inside and put on more comfortable shoes to go walking?" he asked.

Hannah shook her head. "We're not going far. There's a park down the block and across the street. We'll sit on the bench."

Max nodded.

Hannah didn't say anything, just gathered her thoughts as they took in the fresh air. She really appreciated the fact that Max could do silence. Not a lot of people could.

When they got to the small park, they both veered to the one empty bench, and Max cleared off a section and then motioned for Hannah to sit down.

How could Meghan have ever blown this guy off?

"Have a seat," Max indicated. She gave him a small smile then sat down. He looked at his watch. "So we have maybe forty minutes?"

Hannah bit her lip and nodded, she allowed her dark hair to shield her expression. Max sat down and tucked some of the dark strands of her hair back behind her ear.

"Hannah, will you look at me?" he asked hoarsely. She looked up into gray eyes that were the same exact color and shape as Zephyr's; only now, Max's were dark and pleading. "I know that the most important person in all of this is Zephyr. He's got to be devastated at losing Meggie, and I want to be there for him and help ease his pain. But..."

His expression turned to stone.

"But you're mad at Meghan," she finished for him.

Max catapulted off the bench. "Fuck, Hannah. I don't think there has been a word created to describe the kind of fury that is roiling around in my gut," he bit out harshly. He started pacing in front of the bench, and for the first time, Hannah noticed what a big and powerful man Maxwell Hogan was. She knew nothing about him except what she'd learned today. He had to lead a physical lifestyle. He oozed power. He was wearing a cream-colored fisherman's sweater, black jeans that molded to his muscled thighs, and then she noticed again that he was wearing work boots, which had seemed odd when she'd seen them in Elias' office.

Max went on. "If she were in front of me now, I'd be demanding to know what her thinking was. Was there something about me that made her think I would be a bad father? And if there was, what right did she have to make that judgment?"

"Max, no!" Hannah cried out. "I've just met you today,

but I was already wondering why Meghan didn't want to continue seeing you after Tennessee."

He stopped pacing and stared down at her, his eyes pinning her to her seat. "You're not just saying that?"

Hannah shook her head. "You're polite, you're protective, and even now you're trying to get your head on straight about Meghan so you can be there for Zephyr. Then there's how kind and take-charge you were with me in the ladies' room. What? We've known each other for five hours and I know and like more about you than most of the men that I've dated in the last four years."

Max let out a deep breath and sat back down next to Hannah. He picked up her hand between both of his. "Thank you. Thank you for that. This is going to be the hardest thing I've ever done, and in my job, I have to deal with the impossible. Are you willing to be on my team?"

For the first time in hours, Hannah felt hope.

"Do you mean that?"

"Yes I do," was his solemn answer. He looked down at his watch. "We only have twenty-five more minutes. Can you help me understand Meghan?"

"I'll try." Hannah took a deep breath.

11

Hannah's hand felt like ice. "You're cold, should we go inside?" Max asked.

Her beautiful chestnut hair flew around her shoulders as she shook her head. "No, my mother will just interrupt with her own point of view. It won't help."

Max chafed her hand between his, trying to provide some warmth.

She turned her head and pressed her face close to his. "Nobody could have loved Zephyr more than Meghan," Hannah said fiercely. "Nobody. So no matter what else I have to say to you Max, you have to hang on to that, okay?"

Max nodded.

She searched his face and must have seen something that eased her mind because she started talking again.

"Meghan's parents are horrible people. I don't know how in the hell she could have come from Bob and Peggy Lancaster. I met Meghan when I was in third grade when I joined a soccer team in Evanston. My dad had researched the coaches and Mr. Bailey was apparently the best. Dad always wanted the best of everything, so that's why he ended up carting me all the way to Evanston for practice."

"Okay," Max nodded. He really wanted her to hurry this along. He didn't need chapter and verse of their childhood, but if Hannah thought this was important, he'd go with the flow.

"Meghan didn't have any of the gear that the rest of us had, no shin guards or cleats, but she was the best player on the team, so the coach got her some. The other girls knew that he did and they made fun of her. She always came to practice in the same clothes. It took me a while to understand that meant she was poor."

Her bright green eyes burrowed into his, trying to make him understand that what she was saying was important, so he nodded again.

"She always walked to the field for practice. It was close to her house, but when we had games at other schools she sometimes didn't make it. Then Coach Bailey started driving her. One time her dad drove her. He was awful. He yelled at her from the sidelines. He told her to move her fat ass faster, that she fucked up by not getting the ball, and no daughter of his should be such a shitty player."

"How old were the two of you?"

"Eight."

"He actually said that? Yelled that?" Max asked, wanting to make sure of his facts.

Hannah nodded. "The referee stopped the game and tried to throw him out, but he refused to leave until some of the other fathers, including my dad, got involved and forced him back into his car and he drove away."

Max had seen things like this when he was in foster care.

"How did Meghan react?"

"She didn't. She just continued to play. She even made the most goals that game."

"Then what happened?"

Hannah got a wistful look on her face. "My mom and dad came to me after the game like they always did and suggested that I go see if Meghan would like to go to McDonald's with us. They explained to me that I would have to be careful with her, because she might not be used to people being nice to her."

"Your parents sound nice."

"They really are," Hannah smiled at him.

"Anyway, it was like she didn't know what to say. She kept looking at the ground. The coach finally walked over and asked what was going on. When I told him, he persuaded Meghan to go with us." Hannah got that wistful look again. Max waited to see if she would continue. She didn't.

"Hannah?"

"After that, my dad picked Meghan up for all of our soccer games." Hannah shook her head and gave Max a sharp look. "Dad would always go up to Meghan's front door to pick her up, and more times than not, neither of her parents were there to greet him."

"Were there signs of physical abuse?"

"When I was an adult, Mom told me that she'd asked Meghan and she'd said no. Regardless, my dad had called Child Protective Services, apparently so had the coach, but they never built a case to take Meghan out of her home."

"Were there any other relatives?"

"There was her grandmother, the one that Mr.

Peterson talked about, but she was disabled, so she couldn't care for Meghan." Hannah paused.

"I really want you to help me understand why in the world Meghan would have made the decision to not tell me about Zephyr." He swallowed down his anger, or was it grief?

She nodded.

"When Meghan got pregnant, I was living in L.A. I was working for DreamWorks Studios. She was going through the divorce at the same time, there was the restraining order. It was a fucking mess. Mom was there for her, but I came out for three weeks. She told Mom and me that Larry wasn't the father, but she kept mum about who *was* the father. She said she'd think about it after the baby was born."

Hannah shrugged. "I came out again to be with Meghan when she gave birth. Mom had been her birthing coach, but I wanted to be here for the first few weeks after Zephyr was born. That was our first big blow-up. I was pissed that she wasn't going to contact Zeph's father."

Max unclenched his fists. He felt better knowing that someone had been on his side.

"Mom tried to get me to see Meghan's side. She kept telling me about all of Meghan's trust issues." She looked out at the big trees in the park, then back at Max. "I did understand about Meghan's trust issues. Hell, over the years I'd had a front-row seat for the Bob and Peggy Lancaster shit show. For that matter, I still do. But what little Meghan told me about the guy she'd slept with, he didn't seem like the kind of man who deserved not knowing about his son."

"But she never told you who I was?" Max pursued.

Hannah shook her head. "Nope, never. But Max, her

parents were *awful*, and she married Larry Todd when she was seventeen just to get away from them. He was a bastard."

Max nodded. That had been his assessment too.

He closed his eyes and took a deep breath. "I appreciate everything you've just told me. I really do," he said slowly. "If that's all you can give me, then I'll make it work—"

"But you need more," she said tiredly. "You need more of a reason for her to have cut you out of Zephyr's life."

He turned his whole body toward her and again gripped her hands. "God, yes! Please give me something so I can make peace with her decision. So I can always think of her as that loving woman I met in Tennessee as I talk about her to Zephyr throughout the years. I don't want him to know my anger," he pleaded.

"Max, I was Meghan's best friend in the world," Hannah whispered. "She lived for your son. She was working as an accountant when she got pregnant, but as soon as she could she started figuring out a job she could do from home after she gave birth. She finished out her time at the accounting firm and took their maternity leave, but as soon as that ran out she was already working with clients. Meghan was smart like that."

Max looked down at his watch again. "Hannah, I don't mean to rush you, but Zephyr should be waking up from his nap soon."

Hannah nodded. "Max, Zephyr was everything to Meghan. Protecting him and keeping him safe was the most important thing in her whole universe. The first time she let my mother babysit him he was nine months old." Hannah smiled.

"So they're close?"

"Oh yeah. Before I moved here, it was Meghan, Zephyr, and Mom all the way." Then she laughed. "And Dad of course."

"Meghan's parents?"

"They've never met him."

Max gave a satisfied smile.

"When did you move here?" Max asked.

"Fourteen months ago."

"You got a different job?"

"Kind of. I quit DreamWorks and decided to go freelance illustrating fantasy fiction so that I could stay with Meghan and Zephyr after the results of her surgery found that the cancer had spread."

"How bad were things?" Max asked quietly when once again he saw tears glistening on her eyelashes.

"To begin with, not so bad. I just moved into her house so that I could be kind of like the cool aunt who might make a dinner once in a while, you know?"

He didn't, but he nodded.

"It began to be a balancing act. The pain would get to be too much for her to do her job, but then the drugs would make her too loopy to do her job, so she had to give it up. It was a good thing because she could focus more on Zephyr for those last six months. But he was an active three-year-old, and she was tired all the time, so he began to rely more on me. She hated that. He hated that. I hated that."

Max wished like fucking hell he'd been there. Hannah must have seen his reaction.

"You were the sticking point. When Zephyr would sleep, Meghan and I would argue."

"It sounds like I have you to thank for my son," Max said quietly.

Hannah shrugged.

He looked at his watch again. "Do you think he's awake?"

She took a deep breath and gave him a big smile. She stood up and held out her hand to him. "I think it's time for you to come and meet Zephyr."

"Hey, Hannah, I'm ready to go," a young voice called out as soon as Julie opened the front door.

"Why don't you hold on and say hello to..."

A little dark head poked out from underneath her mother's arm. "Who?"

Hannah spun around and looked up at Max frantically, but he ignored her; he was too busy looking down at the little boy. He had wide, curious gray eyes, and Max's heart tipped over into an abyss. He'd thought his world had changed in the lawyer's office, but *this* is when it really changed.

Get your shit together!

"This is my friend Max," Hannah said.

I'm your dad!

Max shook his head. He couldn't say that to the little boy.

Zephyr wiggled in front of Hannah's mom and grinned up at Hannah and Max. "Hiya! My name is Zephyr Maxwell Lancaster. Is your real whole name Maxwell?" he asked as he stared up at Max.

Max cleared his throat and crouched down so he could look Zephyr in the eye. "Yep, my real whole name is Maxwell Russell Hogan. I'm a Lieutenant in the Navy."

"Oh, that's cool."

Max kept staring. Zephyr's hair was black and curly, like his was if he didn't keep it cut short.

Hannah tapped him on the shoulder to get his attention. "Hey, boys, let's go on inside, it's getting kind of cold. Zephyr, you can grab all your stuff and then we'll go home, how does that sound?"

Max stood up straight and watched as Zephyr took off at a run to go back inside.

"We're having chili, right? Are you going to make cornbread?" the boy asked over his shoulder as he ran to get his coat with the Chicago Bears logo on it.

"Yep, you can't have chili without cornbread," Hannah promised him. "And honey butter. Can you go into the kitchen for a minute with Grandma Julie and see if she has any cookies that we can take home?"

"Yay!"

Her mother gave Hannah a knowing look as she cupped Zephyr's head and guided him toward the kitchen.

Max watched them turn the corner. Then Hannah swung her gaze to Max and gripped his arm and swayed against him, her green eyes turning almost black as her eyes dilated.

"What?" he asked. Something was really wrong.

"We didn't talk about what comes next," she gasped. "Nothing. We didn't talk about any of it. What's happening next? Are you flying home tonight? How are you getting to the airport? I've got to get Zephyr back home and get him dinner then put him to bed. But what about tomorrow? And the next day? And the day after?" She was talking fast, he could tell she was panicking.

"Calm down, Hannah, everything's going to be fine," Max soothed. "I'm going to be staying in Chicago. I'll just grab a hotel for a while. We'll figure things out as we go along."

"Can you really do that? You can stay here?"

He put his hand over hers as they dug into the thick sleeve of his sweater. "Absolutely," he said confidently. "I have leave stored up. I'll just call my commander."

"You're not just going to take Zephyr away?"

Max gave her an incredulous look. "God no. That would be insane."

Hannah started to tremble. She swayed forward and he caught her by her arms.

"Steady there."

"This day has been a lot," Hannah mumbled.

"You're talking to the choir."

"She only had oatmeal raisins and those are yuck, so I said no," Zephyr yelled as he came careening into the hallway.

"That wasn't very nice," Hannah admonished.

It was funny to see Hannah go into auto-pilot-Mom.

Zephyr frowned. "She made me take some anyway, cause those are your favorites." He looked up at Max with a frown. "Why are you here?"

"I was going to ask him if he wanted to come to dinner with us tonight."

Max gave Hannah a grateful smile. "I would love to have dinner with you and Zephyr tonight."

"He can't eat all the cornbread, we have to have some for tomorrow," Zephyr commanded.

Hannah sighed. "That wasn't very nice to say either, Zephyr."

"But Hannah, he's h'mongous, he'll eat everything, then we won't have cornbread for breakfast," Zephyr whined.

Max understood that; he didn't like people poaching on his food either. When Hannah caught him grinning, she gave him a slight frown and shook her head.

"Zephyr, what have I told you about being polite?" she asked the boy calmly.

"That it's a good thing," he said looking at the floor. He peeked back up at Max. "I suppose you can't help being really huge. I'll share my food with you," he said reluctantly.

"I appreciate it, Big Guy," Max said as he picked up Zephyr's Iron Man backpack.

"I'm not big, you are, remember?" Zephyr rolled his eyes at him; it was clear he thought Max was stupid.

Max pretended to cough so he could cover up his laughter.

12

"Can you read me one of your books?" Zephyr asked Hannah.

"How about if Max joins us?"

The little boy had been a real pill at dinner. She knew that Max thought Zephyr's acting up was cute, but it wasn't. His rudeness had been getting worse since his mother had left them to go into hospice. It had been Meghan's decision not to let Zephyr see her those last debilitating three weeks before she died, which was another decision that she and Hannah had argued over.

"Is he really going to be here in the morning?" Zephyr demanded to know.

"Yes, Honey, he is."

The moment that Max had asked about a good hotel to stay at, Hannah had realized that having him stay here at the house made the best sense. First, was that having Max get to know Zephyr on his territory made the most sense. Second, she wanted to be on hand to smooth any and everything over for Zephyr, and third, she wanted to make sure that her positive impressions of Max Hogan were right. She prayed to God they were.

"So what book do you want?" Hannah went to the full bookcase in his room. She pulled out three books, one of which was a science fiction book that she had illustrated.

"That one!" he pointed excitedly at *Clara's Galaxy*.

Months ago, Zephyr had seen her working on the illustrations on her computer and he was fascinated to see the actual book in print. Hannah had made up a story to go along with the pictures just for the little boy.

"So can Max come and hear the story?"

Zephyr's lip puffed out in a pout. "No."

She suppressed a grin when she realized there was a tiny part of her that was thrilled to hear that word 'No.' God, she was a mess!

You just invited Max to stay here, you putz!

"Why can't Max come and hear the story?" she asked reasonably.

The psychologist that she'd been taking Zephyr to had explained that Zephyr would naturally cling to her more after Meghan's death. But Hannah had to start integrating Max into the boy's life.

"I don't like him."

"Why don't you like him? Did he do something mean to you?" Hannah really wanted him to try to make sense of his feelings.

She watched as his little brow furrowed. "No. He wasn't mean. He didn't eat all the food," he admitted. "He let me watch the shows I wanted."

"So, he was nice?" she asked gently.

Zephyr nodded.

"Do you think he would like to hear about Clara and

her galaxy? You could help tell the story, I bet he would like it," she coaxed.

Zephyr rolled his eyes and Hannah smothered a laugh. "Okay," he said generously. "He can come listen." Zephyr sat up straight in his bed and hollered Max's name. The kid sure did have a set of lungs.

It didn't take long for Max to appear in the doorway. "You bellowed?" he asked.

"Hannah's going to read us a book. You have to be quiet and listen. I'll 'splain the complicated parts."

Max's eyes twinkled. "Sounds good, Big Guy." Max had been calling him that all night and Hannah knew it was just to see Zephyr roll his eyes, and the kid did *not* disappoint.

Zephyr slapped both of his hands on his bedspread and shook his head in disgust. "*I'm* not big, *you* are. How many times do I need to tell you?"

"Oh yeah, I forgot," Max said as he sauntered into the room. He crouched down next to the bed. "So where should I sit?"

"On the other side of me. Right, Hannah?"

Hannah nodded. She set the other two books on his nightstand and opened Clara's Galaxy.

"This is the book that Hannah made. It's very special, and you're lucky that she's showing it to you. Understand?" Zephyr squinted up at his dad.

"Thanks for explaining, Zephyr," Max said solemnly.

HE WATCHED as she showed Zephyr picture after picture in the big science fiction novel and made up a childish story to go along with it. There were three times that Zephyr stopped her because she had obviously gone off-script and he corrected her; this was a well-worn past time between the two of them. Zephyr struggled to stay awake.

"Don't leave me 'til it's finished," he whispered with his eyes closed.

"I won't, baby," Hannah whispered back.

"Not a baby," he growled softly right before his breathing went into the even pattern of sleep. Hannah kissed his brow. Max could see tears glittering in her pretty green eyes right before she turned off the bedside lamp.

"Come on," she whispered as she rose from her side of Zephyr's bed. She adjusted a little unit, then picked up the accompanying monitor and motioned Max out of Zephyr's room. They went downstairs to the living room.

"A baby monitor?" he asked.

"He's been having nightmares ever since Meghan left."

"Left? Don't you mean died?"

"We had a small service for her, but Zephyr really didn't understand it. What he *did* understand is that close to her death, Meghan hugged him one day and said she was leaving. She left for hospice and never came back. She was on so many painkillers that she could just as well have stayed here, but she didn't want Zephyr to see her like that, so she left. She refused to let me have him come visit. So, to Zeph's mind, she just hugged him good-bye one day and was never seen again."

Fuck! Fuck! Fuck!

Max had seen so many children he'd grown up with in foster care get their heads fucked up, and apparently, Meghan was just one more example.

Hannah turned to him. "Just another thing I wasn't able to talk her out of. The doctors said it was probably all the pain she was in. Two different social workers and Mom and Dad tried to talk her out of her decision. She was just sure it was best for Zephyr. But now he has abandonment issues."

Hannah's movements were jerky as she went over to the kitchen and pulled a bottle of red wine out of the cupboard. Max watched as she fumbled to get the cork out.

"Let me," he said as he took the bottle out of her hand. She turned away from him; he could tell that she didn't want him to see she was crying. She went to another cupboard and grabbed two glasses. He poured them both a glass then took them back out to the living room.

"Coasters?" he asked.

"That's my mother's house, not this house. Just put them on the coffee table."

He did and they sat down next to one another, neither of them picking up their glasses.

"So do you write science fiction?" he finally asked, choosing to change the subject.

She laughed and it made him feel better. She'd been on edge through dinner and storytime so this was good.

"No, I'm not the writing type," she sighed. "Just making up that little fairy tale for Zeph is a stretch for me. Didn't you figure out it is kind of based on Snow White and Jack and the Beanstalk?"

Max's lips twitched. "Now that you mention it. So why did Zephyr say it was your book?"

"I did the illustrations."

"Ahhh," Max nodded.

Hannah picked up her wine glass and took a mouthful then swallowed. Not meeting his eyes, she asked a question. "What do you think of your son?" He could barely hear her words.

He closed his eyes. Image after image after image rushed through his mind. Zephyr smiling, pouting, angry, fierce, joyful.

"He is the most amazing being I have ever met," Max said honestly. "I love him with my whole heart."

When he said those words and looked into Hannah's eyes, he saw a mirror of his own thoughts and feelings. "You understand me, don't you?" he breathed.

She nodded. "Yes." She paused. "I mean no." She took a breath and set down her glass. "It's not like Zephyr is my son, so I could never know what you're feeling." She let her hair fall in front of her face as she looked down at her fingers twisting in her lap. Max reached out and covered them.

"Look at me, Hannah. What do you mean you can't understand what I'm feeling? You love Zephyr, don't you?"

"Of course I do," she burst out as her gaze flew up to stare at him.

"I thought so."

"It's just that he's not mine. He's yours. Yours and Meghan's." Again, she looked down at her lap, only this time he was seeing his big hand covering hers.

"Tell me about him. Tell me what I need to know. Tell me everything," Max pleaded as he tipped her chin up so she would look at him.

"It would take forever. What's more, I've only really known him really well for the past year and a half."

Then she stopped herself and stood up. "Wait a minute," she said with a grin. She rushed over to the shelves near the fireplace and grabbed out an album. "Ta-da!"

She sat back down next to him.

"You're going to love this."

Max turned to the first page of the photo album with reverence, not even noticing when Hannah left the room.

Hannah went up and checked on Zephyr. She hadn't made up the guest room for Max yet, so she pulled out a fresh set of sheets and made the bed. She took a quick swipe at cleaning the bathroom, taking out all of the kid's toys from the bathtub so that Max could take a shower in the morning without killing himself.

She went down to the basement that she had converted to her home studio and started working on a project that was due in a couple of weeks. After she had layered in the background, she noticed that a couple of hours had passed so she went upstairs to check on Max. She found him checking his messages.

"Anything interesting?"

"Nothing that can't wait until tomorrow. I want to thank you for letting me spend the night tonight. You didn't have to do that."

She wandered over to the fridge and pulled out some Entenmann's chocolate cake from the freezer. "Do you like chocolate?" she asked as she held up the box.

"I could be tempted."

"I have vanilla ice cream too."

"Now you're talking."

She dished out dessert and motioned him to the table. She waited until his mouth was full before she started talking. "I'm going to admit to something. I had pretty much come to terms with Zephyr's dad getting custody, otherwise, Elias wouldn't have put off the reading of the will for as long as he did, you know?"

Max just nodded, then he took another bite.

She looked down at her dessert and couldn't bring herself to take a bite. "But even so, my thoughts and emotions are all over the place. Tonight, up in Zephyr's room, when he didn't want you during storytime, I was spitefully happy."

Max's head jerked up to look at her.

"Yeah," she admitted reluctantly. "Talk about illogical since I'm the one who invited you to spend the night and encouraged Zephyr to invite you to storytime." She touched her cheek and felt the pulsing heat there. Thank God the dining room was in semi-darkness so he couldn't see how bright red she must be.

"Jesus, Max, I think that in the last eight hours I've gone completely insane. Just the type of woman you must admire as a guardian for your son."

He put down his fork and pulled her hand away from her face. "Hannah, in the eight hours I've known you, I think that Zephyr has been blessed to have you in his life."

She stared at him in amazement.

13

Max had always prided himself on his ability to get shut-eye no matter what time zone he was in, or what harsh environment he was suffering through, but here he was on a soft mattress with a full stomach and he couldn't get to sleep to save his life. He punched the pillow again. It was no use. He got up and threw on his Navy sweatshirt on top of the sweatpants he was already wearing, snagged his cell phone off the nightstand, and went downstairs to the living room.

It was oh four hundred. Kane had texted him three times yesterday, and he'd ignored all of them. Kostya had texted him too; he wanted to talk about the Commander. He'd better answer that one today. As for Kane? Shit, he fucking *needed* to talk to Kane.

YOU UP?

He sent the text to Kane.

. . .

His phone immediately vibrated with an incoming call.

"How does A.J. feel when you sit around waiting for incoming texts? Isn't she the slightest bit put out?" Max asked.

"You are so out of the loop. A.J. is in Atlanta again. I was waiting around for *her* text, you dumbass," Kane chuckled.

"Well, now that you have me, you're stuck. What's more, I don't even give a shit if A.J. tries to call in; you still have to stay on the line with me," Max demanded.

Kane whistled. "Holy shit, the kid is yours," he breathed out.

"Yep."

"I've got to stay here for a while. Meggie had terminal breast cancer that spread. Shit, Kane, she went through everything, and when I say everything, I mean *everything*."

"How did that impact the kid? Was her family there for her?"

"Her family isn't worth shit," Max answered. "But she's got a surrogate family worth their weight in gold, especially a friend who was like a sister to her. I don't know all of the details yet, but she's been living with Meggie and my son for the last year of Meggie's life. Zephyr adores her."

"Zephyr?" Kane's voice was soft.

"Yeah," Max smiled. "Zephyr Maxwell Lancaster. The attorney said that after a paternity test I can claim him as my own and then he'll be Zephyr Maxwell Hogan."

Kane cleared his throat. "Max, are you sure he's yours?"

"There was a little bit of doubt until I saw him, but he's

a mini-me." Max's grin got wide as he thought of his son sleeping upstairs.

Kane laughed. "Poor kid. What can I do to help?" Kane asked.

"I'm going to talk to Simon tomorrow. I'm going to need to take all my leave."

"Nope," Kane said immediately.

"What are you talking about?"

"Max, this isn't vacation. This is emergency family leave. That's what you would be pushing through for any of us. Simon will be taking care of this for you as soon as you explain the situation."

Max felt himself relax just a tiny little bit. Kane was right. That's exactly what this situation was.

"Now, when are you bringing him home?"

Max slumped forward on the couch, his elbows resting on his knees, the phone up to his ear. "Jesus, Kane, that's the whole fucking problem. For almost a year and a half, Hannah Woods has been playing nurse to Meggie and damn near mom to Zephyr. Meggie considered making Hannah Zeph's guardian, then I would have been completely cut out."

Kane's breath hissed out.

"I don't see a way I can separate the two of them, at least not right away. It's almost like I'll need to set up some kind of custody arrangement."

"If that's what's best for your son, then that's what you do," Kane said decisively. "However, I need a little information on this woman."

"Why? Max asked with suspicion.

"You know damn good and well why. I'm going to do a background check on her."

Max sighed. "You're such a suspicious fuck."

"But you love me."

Max shrugged. "Do the check. But even if there are red flags, I can't separate them; it would psychologically damage him."

"Whoa there. Before you get to that bridge, you've got other steps. There's the DNA testing, there's the paperwork. Where are you staying?"

"I'm with Hannah and Zephyr. Hannah has me in a guest room."

Kane gave a soft whistle. "I have to admit, she sounds solid. How are you getting along with her? I know it was Meghan who decided not to tell you in the beginning, but how is this woman treating you?"

"She'd been trying to get Meggie to tell me about Zephyr from the start. Hannah had no idea who the father was, so today was the first day she heard about me. To my mind, she's been incredibly gracious."

Max looked up the staircase. This time instead of picturing Zephyr, he was picturing Hannah and all of the kind smiles and support she had gifted him with today.

"I'm going to see what I can do to get you into a lab that will fast-track a DNA test for you. You need to get this show on the road," Kane said.

"How long do these things usually take?"

"Fuck if I know, let's just make sure this is fast." Kane paused. "A.J.'s calling through. I'll call you first thing tomorrow and let you know where you're doing your DNA testing at."

"Sounds good," Max said, but the line was already dead so he wasn't sure if Kane had heard him.

He let out a big sigh. *Now*. Now, he felt like he could get some sleep.

"Is he still here?" Max heard Zephyr ask quietly.

"Yes, he's still here this morning, and you're going to be a kind and nice little boy. All of his friends are a long ways away, so it's up to us to make him feel at home."

Max liked the way Hannah tried to explain and coach Zephyr. She'd explained to him last night that the boy had been acting out and being really rude, which was not the Zephyr she was used to. She was hoping that Max would work with her to curb Zephyr's rude behavior and not encourage it. As soon as she'd explained things, he realized he'd have to stop calling the kid 'Big Guy.'

"Where are all of his friends?" Zephyr asked as they started down the stairs.

"He took a plane here from Virginia. We can look on a map and see how far away that is, would that be fun?"

Zephyr jumped over the last step to reach the ground floor.

"Maybe," he answered Hannah. He caught sight of Max. "Hello."

"Good morning, Zephyr," Max said easily.

"What would you two like to eat for breakfast?" Hannah asked.

"Cornbread!" Zephyr said.

"You can have that if you also eat some fruit and yogurt. But you'll have to eat all of your fruit, is it a deal?"

Zephyr scrambled up onto the chair that was clearly his spot at the dining room table. "It's a deal." He turned to Max. "How far away do you live?"

"I live in Virginia. There are three states between Illinois and Virginia," Max said as he went to the fridge. "What can I get the two of you to drink for breakfast?"

"Do you have friends in Ginia?" Zephyr asked.

"He'd like milk, and I'm going to make some coffee," Hannah answered.

Max pointed to the brewed pot of coffee and she smiled. He got down a sippy cup for Zephyr and poured some milk. "Yes, I have friends in Virginia. What about you, do you have friends here? Do you go to school yet?"

"Some days I go to pre-school, but not every day, but I have loads and loads and loads of friends, don't I Hannah?"

"You do, Zeph," she smiled. Max set down the green plastic glass in front of Zephyr then leaned down against the counter to watch Hannah make up the boy's breakfast for him. When she was done cutting up the bananas and strawberries and mixing them up into some vanilla yogurt, she put the bowl in front of Zephyr.

"Where's my cornbread?" he whined.

She raised her eyebrow at him and he ducked his head. "Sorry."

"That's better. I'm glad to see you can hold your horses and stop your whining. I'm bringing the cornbread out to you after I warm it up."

He gave her a bright smile.

God, Hannah is really great with the boy.

Hannah went back into the kitchen and popped a piece of cornbread into the microwave. "What about you, Max, what do you want for breakfast?"

"Why don't you tell me what you want, and I'll get it for you. You did most of the fetching and carrying yesterday."

Her head shot up in surprise.

"Well, all right," she agreed after a moment. She took the bread out of the microwave, cut it into smaller pieces, then slathered it with honey butter. She shook her head as she looked at it.

"What?" he asked.

"Just imagining the mess. This is as bad as when I cook spaghetti."

Max glanced over at the table where there were splotches of yogurt surrounding Zephyr's bowl. "I see what you mean," Max agreed. "Go sit down with him and I'll bring your coffee. Then tell me what you want."

"Okay."

HANNAH WAS AMAZED at how easy the start of the day went. First, the breakfast where Max had served them both up yogurt, coffee, and fruit then cleaned up after Zephyr. Max had already found a place that would fit them in for a DNA test that morning and could have the test results for them by the end of the week.

"How'd you find out about this place?" Hannah asked as they left the clinic.

"One of the guys I work with can find out about damn near anything, so anytime I need something, I ask him."

"Zephyr, watch out, your scarf is going to fall off," Hannah warned the boy. He was running a few yards in front of them, looking for mud puddles to jump in. It was one of his favorite past times.

"What do you do in the Navy? I know that Virginia has a lot of ships and stuff out there. So what's your job?"

"I'm a SEAL."

Her gaze flickered up to look at his face. "Like a Navy SEAL?"

He chuckled. "Yeah, kind of like that."

She looked back and saw that Zephyr's scarf was now in a mud puddle, but before she could snag it, Max had picked it up.

"Yellow light," she yelled out to Zephyr when he got too far away from her. Zephyr went from a run to a walk on the little side street and looked over his shoulder at her.

"I wasn't going to go too far, I promise."

"It was far enough. I needed to catch up." Playing the green, yellow and red light game with Zephyr allowed Hannah a second to think about the fact that Max Hogan was a Navy SEAL. That just never, ever occurred to her.

Absently, she put her hand on Zephyr's silky curls and he looked up at her. "Is it green light now?"

"Sure, green light, but only to that fire hydrant, then it's red light. Deal?" He nodded and dashed off.

When Max started walking, she grabbed his arm and pulled him to a stop. "That's not a very safe job, is it?"

Please let him reassure me.

He glanced over and Hannah followed his eyes. "Zephyr's fine. He knows the rules."

"Hannah, I've been a SEAL for eleven years. I'm thirty-three years old and I'm a lieutenant. I command a team of men."

"But how safe is it?"

He sighed. "I'll admit that it's not like being a dentist, but I'm good at what I do. You also need to know that there are a lot of SEAL team members who have families."

"There are?"

"There are."

She took a breath and walked a little faster to reach Zephyr at the hydrant. "Come on, Honey, let's get you to the car and get you some lunch. Then it's going to be time for your nap."

"Do I have to?" She smiled down at those big gray eyes that melted her heart each time.

"Yeah, you do. But tell you what, how about some SpaghettiOs?"

His eyes lit up. "Dealio!" He turned to Max and grabbed his hand. "We're going to have SpagO's. You'll love 'em. Hurry up, we've got to go home."

"Sounds great, Zeph."

Eleven years. Okay, maybe the job was safer than it looked in the movies.

14

Zephyr hadn't wanted to go down for a nap when Hannah had gotten home from her mom and dad's, but she'd finally convinced him. Max could tell the boy didn't know how to take him—was he a friend or foe? He and Hannah had been waiting for the DNA tests to come back before telling him that he was his dad, but having 'Hannah's friend' staying for a couple of nights made it confusing for the kid. But, it did answer a question Max had; it seemed like neither Meggie nor Hannah had brought over men to spend the night. Not that it should have mattered. It shouldn't have, for fuck's sake. But Max was honest enough with himself to admit it did.

Hannah was in her studio when the text came through, telling Max what he'd already known—Zephyr was his child. He knocked on her open door and she looked up at him from her large computer screen, her ponytail flying.

"Hmmm?" He could tell she was lost in thought. The other-worldly landscape that covered her screen was amazing.

"The text came through," Max said.

"Huh?"

"The DNA test. We can tell Zephyr the truth," Max said as he walked up to her desk.

Her eyes focused and she smiled. "Thank God. Max, he's known something's been up. I'm so glad we can finally tell him."

Then her hands hit her desk with a thud, her smile vanishing.

Max whipped around her desk and crouched down. "What?"

She shook her head and kept looking at her hands.

"Hannah, we're in this together. You've got to let me know."

She sucked in a deep breath then looked up at the open door. He caught on immediately and went to shut it. He didn't want Zephyr walking in on their talk. "Tell me," he prompted as he leaned against the closed door.

She looked up at him from under her lashes. She spoke quietly. "We've been in limbo, waiting for the test. At least I have."

She wasn't making any sense. They'd both known he was Zephyr's father. But he waited so that she could say what she needed to, in her own time. She pushed her chair back from her desk and clutched the arms, her knuckles turning white.

"I...I..."

What in the hell?

Her eyes started to well up with tears. He turned and locked the door as she gulped in a silent sob. He was at her side in a flash.

Her head dropped and her hands lost their grip. Tears streaked down her face and before she had a chance to slide out of her chair he caught her. She was biting her lip so hard he thought she would break the skin. He knew it was to stifle her sob.

"Hannah," he whispered. He turned them so that he was sitting in the chair and she was in his lap. He cuddled her close and she clung to his neck, her silent shudders were heartbreaking.

Shit!

How could they have not talked about this? How could he have not realized that she'd been living on a knife's edge?

"Hannah, you're not losing him," he whispered harshly. She wasn't hearing him. Her grief was absolute.

Max pulled her arms away from his neck, trying to tilt her face up so she could look at him, but her eyes were shut tight.

"Look at me, Hannah."

Her head shook so wildly, her hair came out of her ponytail.

"Hannah!" He gripped her chin, forcing it up. "Look at me. You're not losing him. I promise you. He needs you. You're not losing him."

She tried to pull away from his hold and turn to the door. "He'll wake up soon," she gasped. "He can't see me like this. He'll get upset." Hannah's voice sounded like she'd swallowed broken glass.

"Hannah, did you hear me? You're not going to lose him."

She started to struggle. "I need to clean up."

"Everything's going to be fine," Max said soothingly.

Hannah shoved at him violently. "How! How can it be fine?" she shrieked softly. "How can it ever be fine again?" She stumbled off the chair and shoved the heels of her hands into her eyes. He would have pulled her into his embrace, but she lurched across the room and sagged against the door.

"Oh God, I'm so sorry Max," she whimpered.

He stalked her carefully as she tried valiantly to pull herself together.

How had he fucked up so badly? How?

"Zephyr needs you. I know that. How could you ever think that I would pull the two of you apart?"

She was mere inches away from him and he once again pulled her into his arms. He breathed a sigh of relief as she fell against his chest, but she was still softly keening in pain. She hadn't heard him.

He bent his knees and cupped her cheeks, willing her to open her eyes.

"Hannah," he kissed her forehead. "Look at me." He pressed a kiss to her temple. "Please, Baby, look at me."

Her eyes fluttered open.

"I was going to talk to you about this. I swear to God, I was going to talk to you about this. I got so excited about being able to tell him about being his dad, I didn't think about how we would work things out."

"Talk about what?" the words tumbled out of her mouth.

"Right now it's important for him to stay here. He has you, he has your parents, he has this house. I've talked to my commander. I'm taking emergency family leave. We're going to figure this out."

"But eventually you have to go home to Virginia," she whimpered.

"Zephyr is my priority. He's our priority. I'm staying."

She threw her arms around his neck. "Oh my God,

Max. Do you mean it?" Her beautiful green eyes beamed up at him.

Her eyes shimmered, her lips were wet with her tears.

"Yes," he said hoarsely.

"Max," his name was a mere whisper, and he was lost.

He bent his head and brushed his lips against hers, testing, tasting.

Hannah parted her mouth hungrily, her fingers speared into his hair, her fingernails scoring his scalp. He feathered his tongue along Hannah's lips, but she was having none of it. She suckled him deeper and an overwhelming need roared through him in response.

Max did what he'd been wanting to do for two days. He played with her thick, silky hair, then pulled it back so he could kiss her deeper as his other arm pulled her closer. She was warmth and beauty in his arms—not just physical, but so much more. She yanked away from him and a sense of pain began to form when he too heard small feet stamping down the stairs and Max smiled.

MAX FINISHED HEATING up the dinosaur pasta while Hannah freshened up. He and Hannah had talked about how to broach the 'daddy' talk with Zephyr, and it sounded good, so she was going to take the lead.

"Max, is it done yet?"

"Yep."

The microwave dinged, letting him know that last night's eggplant parmigiana was also done. Max got everything dished up and on the table by the time Hannah was back to get the drinks. He settled down at the table and picked at his food as he watched Zephyr plow through his SpaghettiOs.

"Can we play t-ball before it gets dark?" he asked, looking between the two of them.

"Sure," Hannah answered, "but first, Max and I want to talk to you about something."

Zephyr cocked his head. "About what?"

"Do you remember asking why you didn't have a dad like some of your other friends at pre-school?" Hannah asked him.

"No."

"It was after they had field day and there were all of the father-son games, remember?"

Zephyr frowned. "I don't remember."

Hannah gave Max a helpless glance.

Max got up from his seat at the dining room table and crouched down beside Zephyr so that they were eye to eye. He lightly rested his hand on the little boy's shoulder. "Do you know why your mom named you Zephyr Maxwell?" Max asked quietly.

The little boy shook his head, his eyes wide.

"It's because she named you after me. I'm your dad, Zephyr."

"Really?" the boy whispered his question.

Max felt the burn of tears and he forced them back, not wanting Zeph to think this was a bad thing. "Being your daddy is the best thing in my life. I am so glad I finally found you. I love you so much."

Zephyr looked over at Hannah for confirmation and Max saw her nod. His eyes got even wider as he looked back at Max.

"How'd you get lost?"

"I was far away in Virginia," Max explained. "Your

mommy and I couldn't find one another, but when she died she made sure that I could find you."

Zephyr's face crumpled and he turned back to look at Hannah. "I don't want Mommy died."

Hannah put her arm around Zephyr. "I know you don't, Sweetheart."

Max watched as one lonely tear streaked down his son's face and he kicked himself for saying that Meghan had died. As if she knew what he was thinking, Meghan looked over Zephyr's head and mouthed, "Not your fault."

"Do you want to talk about your mom or look at pictures?" She stroked his hair as he cuddled closer, but as he did he turned to look at Max.

"You knew Mommy?" he asked.

"I did," Max said solemnly. "Your mom was a beautiful lady."

"She got sick," Zephyr told him from the comfort of Hannah's arms.

"I know."

Max watched as Zephyr's gray eyes continued to contemplate him. "Are you going to go away?"

"No, Zephyr, I'm not," Max promised as he held out his hand.

Zephyr's chubby little fingers grasped his and he smiled. "Good."

HANNAH HEARD the printer whirring as she walked upstairs from her office. It was eleven o'clock at night, was Max still at it?

Warm gray eyes smiled at her when she made her way

into the dining room. "Did you send off everything to Dickerson?" Max asked.

Hannah stretched her neck. "Finally." She surveyed the dining room table. "It looks like even more paper than last night, how is that even possible?" She went to the fruit bowl and saw that Max had filled it up when he went grocery shopping. "Want me to cut up some peaches?" she asked.

"Sounds good. I'm about ready to pack it in. I'll meet you at the couch."

Hannah pulled three peaches out of the bowl and went about peeling and slicing. By the time she was done adding a little bit of sugar and cream the dining room table was barren and Max was scrolling through his smartphone on the couch. She handed him his bowl and sat down on the other side of the couch from him.

Max set down his bowl of fruit, then went to the fireplace and clicked it on. When he came back he settled down next to her before picking up his bowl again. He gave her a half-smile, his eyes twinkling. "It's cold tonight, we need to conserve body heat."

This was the first kind of intimacy since their kiss ten days ago, and Hannah wasn't sure how to take it. Since Max hadn't touched her or talked about it since, she'd put it down as a one-off. But what about now?

She watched as he slowly ate his fruit. "Don't you like yours?" he finally asked.

Hannah started when she realized her bowl was still full. She took a bite. "Yeah, it's good."

Max laughed.

Ah shit, he knows.

"I'm sorry about all the paperwork you're having to do," Hannah said.

"Honey, you've said that every single day," he admonished softly. "You weren't able to do it because you weren't named Zephyr's guardian. It's fine, I'm getting through it," he assured her again.

"How can you say that? It looks so overwhelming."

Max's white teeth gleamed in the firelight as he grinned. "Hannah, I work for the United States government, doing paperwork is in my blood."

She laughed. "Nu-uh, you're a Navy SEAL, pull the other one."

"Are you going to eat that?" Max nodded toward her half-finished bowl.

"No."

He placed both of their bowls on the coffee table, then put his arm around her shoulders. "I don't know what all you've been reading about my job, but I'm an officer. Let me tell you, paperwork is part and parcel of what I do. What's more, it better be done right the first time, or I'm stuck with numerous reworks and delays."

"Did you go into the Navy knowing you wanted to be an officer?" Hannah asked.

Max nodded. "I didn't have much control when I was growing up. As a matter of fact, I didn't have any. I was in the foster care system. I was determined to do something when I got out of the system that would give me control."

"Can I ask you questions about your childhood, or is that something you don't like to talk about?"

Max picked up one of her hands resting in her lap and placed it against his chest. "I wouldn't have brought it up if I wasn't comfortable discussing it with you."

15

Hannah's fingers kneaded against his chest and the sensation went straight to his cock. Fuck, he'd been thinking about doing this for the last three days. If he hadn't been getting in fifteen-mile early morning runs each day, there wouldn't have been a chance in hell he would've gotten the few hours of sleep he'd been getting each night.

She let out a sharp gasp and pulled her hand away.

"Don't stop," Max pleaded. "Zephyr's asleep."

"That's not it, do you really think this is a good idea?" Her green eyes bored into his.

Max cupped her face and touched his lips to hers. He savored her moan, then he lifted his head. "You feel it too."

She gently pulled his fingers from his face. "I have never, ever, felt so attracted to a man in my life," she softly admitted.

"Thank God," Max said as he touched his forehead against hers. "But, Hannah, I don't want you to think I haven't thought about this. I have. Ten days ago was a fluke, a beautiful, wonderous fluke." He lifted his head to stare into her eyes. "But tonight? This is something I *have* thought about." He rolled his eyes like Zephyr. "Scratch that, it's something I've obsessed about. I would never do anything that could jeopardize our relationship because it would crush the little boy we both adore."

She breathed out a sigh of relief and smiled. "Exactly."

"Baby, you're not hearing me. When I say I've thought this through, I mean I've thought this through. I've never lived with a woman before. But for almost three weeks, twenty-four-seven, I've lived with you, and I couldn't have found a better woman to be spending my hours with."

Hannah pulled back, scared. How often had she thought the same thing?

"It's because of Zephyr," she argued quickly. "You're just drawn to me because I'm a mother figure to your son," she dismissed him.

"Do you think that I'm really that dumb?" he asked calmly.

"Of course not," she jumped in. "You're one of the smartest men I've met."

It was true too. Max wasn't just book smart, he was emotionally smart. She'd never met anyone in the world like him.

"Hannah, I haven't told you much about my job or my training. I'm used to quickly assessing situations and making life and death decisions. It's what has kept me and my men alive."

She shivered at his words. She reached up to touch his

chest again, but this time with both of her hands. She had to feel his warmth. He covered her hands with his.

"Honey, I didn't tell you this to scare you. I'm telling you this so that you know that when I say I've thought about something, I've looked at it from all angles, and I have. I would never do anything that would jeopardize Zephyr's emotional security. Do you believe me?"

She did. "I do."

"Hannah, this isn't about me not being able to keep my hands off of you, this is about the fact that my heart has become involved. And no, not because of who you are to Zephyr. This is about who you are becoming to me." He tilted her chin up and kissed the tip of her nose. Kissed her lips. "Who I think you are destined to become to me."

Hannah gasped. "Max, that's not possible. What you're saying's not possible," she choked out her denial.

He gave her a crooked grin. "Be honest with me, Hannah. Really, really honest. If Zephyr weren't involved, would we be in bed right now?"

"Well, yeah," she spit out with a laugh. Then she sobered. She pushed away from him and stood up, well aware of the fact that he let her. She walked over to the fireplace and for long minutes she stared into it.

"Are you coming back to me?" he asked gently.

She went back and sat down with more space between them.

"I can't do this right now," she whispered. "I can't stand the idea of Zephyr being hurt, and eventually this will hurt him."

Max smiled calmly, not touching her. "I understand that's what you're thinking, *now*. But can you do me a favor?"

She nodded.

"I'm a few days ahead of you on this," Max said. "Can you look into your heart and see if you think we might have a chance? I'm not talking about some kind of affair. I'm talking about a relationship that could last forever."

Hannah's chin wobbled.

"You love me?" she asked.

"I absolutely do love you. You're an amazing woman who I will always cherish," he said immediately.

She felt a tear drip down her cheek.

"But, I'm beginning to fall *in* love with you, Hannah. The kind of love that has the potential to rip out my heart and leave me bleeding by the side of the road."

God, the amount of emotion in his words about killed her. She'd never had any man talk to her like this.

"But Hannah, with our situation, with who we both are to Zephyr, I'm doing my damndest not to fall unless you're going to be with me. That's why I'm trying to be direct about this, and see where you are." He blew out a breath. "Where you *could* be," he whispered with a small smile.

More tears fell.

How could she *not* be in love with this man? How?

"Max—" she started.

"No, Hannah." He put two fingers against her lips. "You take some time to think about this. *Really* think about this. Even if you say yes, it won't be to forever, it would be to seeing if we have the potential for forever."

She desperately needed to kiss this man, but instead, he got up and picked up the two bowls. He took them to the kitchen, put them in the dishwasher, and started it up.

"Good night, Hannah."

"Good night, Max."

"What's up, Buttercup?" Julie called out to her daughter as she walked into the house. "Where's Zephyr?"

"I left him with Max," Hannah said when she stepped into her mom's kitchen. "Do you have cookies?"

Julie lifted one finely arched brow. "How many do you need?" she asked carefully.

"Every single one that you've baked," she said as she plopped down at the table. Hannah had no intention of telling her mother what Max had said two nights ago. She adored her mother, but on something like this, she'd keep her own counsel. However....

"Do you need some ice cream with those cookies?" Julie asked as she got down the smallest stainless steel mixing bowl. Oh thank God, her mother wasn't going to skimp.

"Yes, I need ice cream. Can you heat up the cookies?" Hannah practically begged.

Julie took two handfuls of cookies out of the crystal cookie jar and put them on a paper towel and inserted them into the microwave. Then she went to the freezer and took out a half-gallon of vanilla ice cream and pulled out her ice cream scooper. When the microwave dinged, she placed the cookies into the bowl, then scooped the ice cream on top and placed the decadent dessert in front of Hannah, who just stared at it.

"Well, you're not crying, so Max isn't taking Zephyr away. You're not eating yet, so you haven't had wild monkey sex—"

"Mom!" Hannah shouted out, appalled.

"Hey, I remember Clive when you were a junior at Northwestern. You gained seven pounds. Three years later when we shared those two bottles of wine, it sure sounded to me like it was wild monkey sex."

Hannah hit her forehead against the dining room table. "I'm never drinking with you again."

"Yeah, I think that might be a good idea," Julie said drily.

Hannah picked up her spoon and took a bite. "This is good."

"I'm glad. Now, do you want to tell me what's going on?"

"Not really." Hannah took three more bites while her mother watched her with a half-smile on her face.

"Did you come for advice?" Julie asked.

Hannah put down her spoon. "I think Max is a dumbass," she said.

Julie shrugged. "He has a penis, it goes with the territory."

Hannah snorted.

"Have you seen his penis?"

"Mom!" Hannah knew her face was the color of a tomato.

"I'd have to be blind if I didn't notice the sparks flying between the two of you last week."

Hannah picked up her spoon again and shoveled down another five hundred calories.

"Why is he a dumbass?" Julie asked.

"Actually, he might be really smart, and trying to use me." Hannah took another bite then swallowed. "But I don't think so, he's just too damn honorable. I really think he's scared, so he's glomming onto me."

"With his penis?" Julie deadpanned.

"Jesus, Mom!"

"What can I say, I might have noticed he's hot." Julie

pulled the bowl away from Hannah and grabbed both of her hands. "Are you falling for him?"

"I think I really am, and it's the stupidest thing I've ever done in my whole life. Even stupider than monkey sex with Clive." Hannah groaned. "Wait, even stupider then *telling* you about monkey sex with Clive."

"What about him? What is he feeling?" her mother asked her gently.

"That's what I was saying. I think he's a dumbass and can't figure things out about his feelings because he just needs me for Zephyr. But, Mom, I want him to want me for me," Hannah's voice trickled off.

"Of course you do, Honey. Do you know how much your father and I like this man?"

Hannah shook her head.

"We like him a lot. We couldn't ask for a better man for our quasi-grandson." She gripped her daughter's hands tighter before releasing them and then taking a dainty bite out of the bowl and swallowing. "He's a good man, Hannah," she whispered.

"What do I do?" Hannah begged to know.

Julie opened her mouth and Hannah held up her finger in warning.

"I promise, I wasn't going to mention his penis," Julie's eyes twinkled.

Hannah sighed. It didn't matter, because she knew damn good and well that Max's penis was definitely going to be part of her future.

"They've retained an attorney," Elias Peterson said.

"I had no idea they could afford one," Hannah said

with disgust as she looked out the kitchen window into the backyard and watched Max show Zephyr how to use a baseball mitt. "You didn't tell Max, did you?" she asked the old man anxiously.

"I wanted to talk to you first. Have you told him about Bob and Peggy's harassment?"

She hadn't. To begin with, it had never occurred to her because she was so used to handling things on her own. But after overhearing Max ream out someone named Nic for not telling him about a problem he was having she knew she was going to be in deep shit for not having told him about Meghan's parents. The man was a little overprotective.

Hannah grabbed a bottle of water and pulled out the Tylenol bottle from the cupboard. She shook out three pills and winced when she saw that the water bottle was empty. She ended up swallowing the pills dry.

"No, I never really talked to Max about it," Hannah admitted. "But, Mr. Peterson, they've never met Zephyr; how could they have any kind of case to secure guardianship?" she asked.

"They really can't. But they can make things difficult, and they can tangle up things in the courts. What's more, they have an attorney who is known for taking cases like this on contingency, so she will fight this if she thinks there is money to be made."

"Oh for God's sakes," she bit out, "CPS was called against them for how they raised Meghan, how could they have a leg to stand on to take Zephyr? Anyone with eyes could see they just want Meghan's life insurance money!"

Hannah's stomach began to rebel. She hadn't eaten anything today, it was hot, and she'd taken the pills.

I'm a dumbass!

She saw Max and Zephyr start to head in.

"Hannah, I'm going to have to inform Max what's going on later today. This was a courtesy call to you."

Oh, fuck.

"Thanks, Mr. Peterson, I appreciate it. I'll have him give you a call this afternoon."

"Thank you," he said before he hung up.

The backdoor burst open and Zephyr skidded across the kitchen floor as he practically fell against her. "I'm going to be the bestest player in t-ball! Max, I mean, Dad, knows everything!" Zephyr yelled.

Hannah touched his little head and smiled down at him, then up at Max. It always gave her a thrill when Zephyr called Max, Dad.

"Tell you what, you go take off your shoes, wash your hands, and you get a half-hour of tablet time. How does that sound?"

Zephyr's eyes practically bugged out of his head. "For real?"

"Yep," Hannah assured him.

Zephyr sat down right in front of her and pulled off his shoes, then threw them near the backdoor as he zoomed up the stairs.

Max frowned as he looked at her. "What's wrong?"

Hannah reached around him, grabbed the package of English muffins, pulled one out, and took a bite.

"Did you forget to eat?" he asked. Then he picked up the bottle of Tylenol. "Do you have a headache?"

Hannah nodded.

He led her out to the sofa and she sank into the cushions. "Now, this isn't a project, so tell me what in the hell is going on."

Hannah took another bite out of the dry muffin.

"Fuck!"

Max whirled to the kitchen and came back in two minutes. He yanked the muffin from her fingers and handed her a plate with a ham sandwich. "Eat." After she swallowed her first bite, he handed her the glass of apple juice he was holding and handed it to her. "Swallow."

The process continued until she had eaten half of the sandwich.

When her stomach was feeling a little better she looked up at him. She easily read his expression. She knew a lot of people might think he was angry, but she knew that he was scared and concerned.

"I'm better now," she assured him as she put the dishes down.

He sat down next to her and wrapped his arms around her. "Talk."

She snorted out a laugh.

"Hannah, there is nothing funny going on," he growled.

"Actually, there kind of is. I believe the last three words you'd said to me were; eat, swallow, talk. You were kind of sounding like Tarzan."

"Hannah, enough with the shit. Tell me what the fuck is going on."

Okay, maybe a little mad, she admitted as she looked into his stormy gray eyes.

"I screwed up, Max. I should have been telling you about Meghan's parents." She shrugged out of his protective hold and went over to the counter to get her phone out of her purse. She brought it back and unlocked it. "Here are the texts I've been getting from Peggy ever since Meghan died."

Ice coalesced throughout Max's body as he read each escalating text. There were twenty-seven—he'd counted.

"This first one came two days after Meghan died?" Max clarified.

Hannah nodded.

YOU HAVE NO RIGHT TO TAKE MY GRANDSON AWAY FROM ME, I'LL HAVE YOU PROSECUTED FOR KIDNAPPING.

The one that came in three days ago was the worst.

ZEPHYR WOULD BE BETTER OFF DEAD THAN LIVING WITH SOMEONE WHO HATED HIS MOTHER SO MUCH. I'M GOING TO MAKE SURE HE'S TAKEN AWAY FROM YOU.

"Is this all?" Max gritted out the question.

"No," Hannah admitted. "Today I got my one and only text from Meghan's dad." She took the phone from his hands and pulled up that text.

I HAVE PROOF YOU KILLED MY DAUGHTER, YOU WILL PAY.

. . .

"And you've been ignoring this? Why didn't you go to the police when they first started coming in?" Max demanded to know.

"I was stupid, Max," she said tiredly as she looked up at him. "Meghan got stuff like this all the time. She was constantly blocking their numbers, getting new numbers, then blocking them again. But finally, after having Max, she had to keep the same number, so then they would call and text from different phones. You just get numb to it."

"No," Max said as he glared at her phone, then looked up at her. "No, you never get numb or put up with this kind of abuse."

Hannah bent her head, her hair covering her chalk-white face.

Ah shit, there's more.

"Elias Peterson said they've retained an attorney to try to gain custody," Hannah whispered.

Max let loose a short laugh. "Are you fucking kidding me?"

Hannah shook her head.

"That isn't even a thing," he scoffed.

"Mr. Peterson said it could make things difficult for us." Hannah paused, then looked up at him. "I'm not sure, but I think it would really be a problem if you would want to take him to Virginia. You'd want to do that eventually, wouldn't you?"

Max kneaded the back of his neck.

"We're just taking this one day at a time, remember?" he said gently.

"But your job is there," she persisted. "Your emergency leave can't last forever. Are you saying you want to quit and move to Chicago?"

Max held her stare. "No, I don't. That's part of why I talked to you the other night."

Her heart plunged.

Am I right? Is he just trying to reel me in and use me?

Max looked back down at her phone. "I need to forward this to my second in command. Kane is the one who handles all of my computer stuff."

"Okay, do whatever you want," she said listlessly. "But what kind of help will that be?"

"I'm not sure yet," Max admitted. "But it's a start."

Hannah got up from the table. "Elias Peterson wants you to call him. I'm going up to see how Zephyr is doing."

Max reached out for her arm as she tried to pass by. "Hannah, don't do this," he begged.

"Do what?"

"Don't think that because I want to eventually take Zeph to Virginia that that's the reason I am determined to explore what's between us."

Hannah shrugged him off. "You need to call Elias."

16

"Sounds like you totally fucked that up," Kane said.

Max kneaded the back of his neck as he held his smartphone to his ear. "Thanks for pointing out the obvious. Now tell me what you think about the texts."

"Meghan's parents are whacked."

"Again, Kane, you're all about the obvious today. You're so helpful."

"No, I mean seriously whacked. Nothing on the books, no convictions, which is pretty fucking unfortunate. Instead, you have got one con after another, with one victim after another."

"I don't get it," Max said as he leaned against the back porch railing and looked out into the darkness. "If they've conned all of these people, why no records?" he asked tiredly.

"They also ran a pawnshop that the cops were sure was a front for laundering money, but they never were able to prove it. But they were so goddamned stupid, even doing that they ran it into the ground and had to close it four years ago," Kane said in disgust.

"Okay, what else?"

"They were constantly taking advantage of people who were in the shadows. People who didn't want to have anything to do with the cops. Time and time again they would find someone on Craig's List who listed their car, then send them a cashier's check over the amount of the price. They would then say that an error had been made and that after the cashier's check had been deposited, that the seller please wire them back the overage on the day they picked up the car. Well, of course, the cashier's check would never really clear, and they'd be out the car, and the extra amount they'd wired to the soon-to-be-closed checking account."

Max shook his head. "How'd you find out?"

"It's a typical scam; when I saw how many accounts they'd opened with so many banks I did some tracking. They've been pulling this one for nine years."

"They've squatted more than a few times, but always under different aliases. I don't think they've paid rent in the last eighteen years."

"Where are they living now?" Max asked.

"Oh well, now, they've cleaned up their act. Their current attorney has fronted them some cash so they'd look good to a judge. They're in a two-bedroom apartment in Whiting. They just moved in three weeks ago."

"Can you prove the money came from the attorney?" Max asked.

"Not in a way that a court will like," Kane admitted.

"Fuck."

"So what are you going to do with the mess you've made with Hannah?" Kane asked.

"She and I have never been on a date. We need some grown-up time together to talk about grown-up things."

"Okay," Kane said slowly. "I'll bite. How are you going to get her to see that you wanting her to move to Virginia with you isn't just to take care of Zephyr."

Max blew out a frustrated breath. "That's the fucking problem. Until we have some time together and see that if we really have something, I'm not going to suggest that Hannah uproot her life and follow me to Virginia."

"So instead, you're just going to basically rip her kid out of her arms?" Kane asked conversationally.

Max thought his head was going to explode. "No, goddammit, no!"

"So, you admit that you're getting together with her so you can keep the three of you together?"

Max squeezed his phone so hard it was a wonder it didn't shatter into pieces.

"Max," Kane said softly. "I'm just trying to point out how Hannah is viewing all of this."

"So tell me how to solve this."

"You told me what you said to her the other night, and you were a fucking pussy."

"Huh?"

"You either love her or you don't. What the hell is this, 'I'll choose to fall in love with you' bullshit? A.J. would have had my balls in a vice if I'd said something so pathetically stupid to her."

Max winced. Hearing Kane spit his words back at him, he had to agree. Had his background really fucked him up so badly that he was that scared of being hurt? Of taking a chance?

"I've got to go," Max said.

"Yeah you do," Kane agreed.

Hannah had been bracing for Max since yesterday's blow-up. Today she'd taken Zephyr to pre-school so that they could have some adult together-time to talk and she'd taken the long way home, hoping she could get her head on straight before she saw him.

Max opened the front door as soon as she pulled into the driveway.

He looked so damned good. He was wearing the light blue Henley shirt that emphasized all of his muscles. Did he have to be wearing that when she needed to stay strong? She pulled her phone out of the charger and remembered he was going to want to talk about Meghan's damned parents and she winced.

She turned off the car and reached for her purse and phone. Max opened the driver's side door for her. "I was worried about you," he said huskily.

"No need," she assured him, without looking at his face.

He pulled her purse out of her hands and shut the car door behind her as he walked with her up the porch steps and ushered her inside. "Are you hungry?" he asked.

"No, it's too early for lunch."

Max nodded in agreement. "We need to talk."

Finally, Hannah did look up at him. "God, Max, I'm sorry for being so stupid. I should have warned you about Bob and Peggy so long ago." She desperately wanted to beg him not to be mad at her, but that was stupid. He either would be or wouldn't be. But please, could he not be?

"Hannah, we're past that."

She frowned. "That easy? Are you sure?"

"Yeah. I promise you, they are not going to do

anything to harm Zephyr or his life. We're not going to allow it."

"You and Elias?"

"You and *me*," Max corrected with a slow smile. "Okay, I might have some of my buddies from my team help too. But, we're not going to put up with a damn thing from those scum-sucking bottom feeders."

Hannah felt herself calm just a tiny little bit. At least about that. "So, if we're not talking about Meghan's parents, are we talking about Virginia?"

Max nodded. "How about we not just stand in the middle of the living room, huh?" He tugged at her trenchcoat. "Can I help you out of that?"

She nodded. He hung up her coat for her and then she went over to the armchair that was next to the couch. Max sat on the corner of the couch closest to her without making a verbal comment, but he did raise his eyebrow. Hannah didn't care, she wasn't going to be pressured.

He sat forward, his elbows resting on his knees. "Hannah I want to explain—"

She held up her hand. "You have nothing to explain. You want what's best for Zephyr. Full stop. How could I ever fault you for that?"

"Yes, I do. But for the record, I'm more than capable of having multiple high-level priorities in my life," he said sardonically.

She shot him a grim smile. "Maybe you can. But are you telling me that anything would ever be as high as Zephyr?"

His eyes turned molten silver. "If I had a wife. If I had another child. Then yes."

She sat back in the chair as if she'd been shoved.

"You think you might have more kids?"

"I never intended to have children unless I found and married the woman I loved." He grimaced. "So that one was shot out of the water, but here I am, fucking ecstatic about it."

Hannah grinned. "Yeah, I'm pretty happy that condom failed too, I can't imagine a world without Zephyr in it."

"Okay, so we're in agreement on that." Max leaned closer and blew out a breath. She felt surrounded by him and she was beginning to melt. "Hannah, it's been pointed out to me that the other night I was talking out my ass."

"I don't understand."

He placed a hand on each arm of her chair, effectively closing her in. "I bet you don't understand, because I sure as hell didn't."

Max's mouth hovered over hers. "Let me be perfectly clear about something. If I felt I needed someone to take care of Zephyr when I eventually move back to Virginia, Meghan's life insurance is going to make it easy for me to find one hell of a nanny. Or, I could just as easily pay for a damned duplex for the two of us so you could live on one side and I could live on the other and Zephyr would have us both forever. Money works wonders that way, you know?"

His eyes glowed as she tried to make sense of all he was saying.

"Do you understand what I'm saying, Hannah? When I tell you that I'm in love with you, it's not because I need a caretaker for Zephyr, or that I don't want the two of you to be apart from one another. I'm pretty sure I can still make those things happen. Are you hearing me?"

Her eyes widened. "You'd buy a duplex?"

"Fuck yeah. This is our boy I'm talking about. But there's a problem with that idea."

"What?"

His right hand lifted up and circled her neck, his thumb pressed against the flutter in her neck. "Your pulse is racing wildly. It always does when I get close." Max lowered his hand, letting it drift over her breast where her needy nipple poked against his palm. "And here, when I'm close, your nipples are always so tight."

He picked up her hand from her lap and placed it over his groin, and she felt the bulge of his erection. "And this has been me for what seems like forever," he groaned.

She shook her head. "It's just sex," she protested as her hand caressed him through his jeans.

"No, it's not, Hannah." He cupped her face. "Tell me who I am to you."

Nooooooo! That's such an unfair question.

"Okay, I'll tell you who you are to me," he said as if he heard her protest. "You're Hannah Woods, the woman I admire most in this world. The woman who is currently breaking my heart because she's sitting here confused and hurting. The woman who wants to help everyone she knows. A loving mother, a talented artist, and the woman that I'm in love with."

He meant the words. She could see the love shining from his eyes, like shards of starlight piercing her soul.

"God, Max. I can't believe you just said all that."

She felt tears coming, and then they fell. "Please tell me I'm not crying again," she begged him.

He chuckled as his thumbs brushed away her tears. "You're not crying."

"Liar."

He shrugged. She must have bitten her lip, because his thumb pulled it from her teeth, then started to caress it. Hannah felt that caress deep in her belly.

"Can you tell me how you feel, Hannah?"

"I started to fall in love with you when you brushed off the bench at the park that first day," she admitted. "But I knew it was hopeless and wrong."

"Not hopeless. Not wrong."

"God, I love you so much, Max Hogan."

His lips hovered above hers and she drew back. She pushed strongly against his chest. "Sit back down on the couch."

He sat back and gave her his full attention.

"I know kids are resilient," Hannah said. "Zephyr is a testament to that."

Max nodded.

"My gut. My heart. My head. Everything believes all that you've told me," she said quietly.

"But?" he asked slowly.

"No buts," she smiled. "I believe you. I believe you mean them...now."

His smile turned wide. "So that's it. Okay, I see where you're going with this. You're worried that things might change and Zephyr will get caught in the crosshairs."

"Exactly." She was so relieved he got it.

"Hannah, I believed it when you told me that you loved me," he smiled. "What's more, I believe it's going to be a forever kind of love."

She leaned forward and dropped her head onto his chest. "Fuck, you know how to mess with my heart."

Max stroked her hair and waited for what she was going to say next. She finally sat up and looked at him. "When do you need to go back to Virginia?"

"I want to get all of the medical expense paperwork taken care of, and all this shit with Meghan's parents, I'm thinking a month."

"Okay. A month then. We give this relationship a month and see where it goes. In the end, I'm moving to Virginia no matter what. My job is portable and there is no way I'm not going to live close to Zephyr."

Max stroked a hand from the top of her knee up to the apex of her thighs. "Oh, I know where this relationship is going," he murmured with a wicked smile.

Hannah stood up. "My bed is better than the guest bed."

17

"How come you make Zephyr make his bed if you don't make yours?" Max asked as he peeked into her bedroom for the first time.

"Oh for goodness sake, all he has to do is pull up his comforter," Hannah laughed. "It's good for him. Especially after Meghan died, he needed even more of a sense of normalcy. He wasn't doing well when I just let things slide."

Max nodded. He'd noticed that each week he'd spent here, Zephyr had become less rude, more relaxed, and kinder. Hannah's way of dealing with him definitely garnered results. He watched as she picked at her comforter and tried to smooth it out, her hand trembling.

What the hell?

He took three steps and pulled her into his arms. "Your room is beautiful, just like you are."

"Don't you mean we're both a mess?" she breathed up at him.

"You're going to find out that I say what I mean. You're beautiful, Hannah Woods." His hand snaked behind her head and yanked out the scrunchie that kept her hair in a ponytail. He grinned as her hair fell down below her shoulders. "I love your hair."

"You don't seem to like my ponytails."

"I don't," he agreed. He raked his fingers through her chestnut tresses, loving how the sunlight picked up all the different colors like red, orange, and caramel. "You have gorgeous hair. It goes perfectly with your eyes. Your skin."

Hannah's cheeks flushed and he could see that he'd surprised her. Shit, he really hadn't told her how beautiful she was to him. That was going to change. Now.

"I have never had a more stunning woman in my arms," he whispered as he lifted her chin and feathered a kiss across her lips.

"Max." He heard the dispute start, and he muffled it with the kiss that he'd been dying for. She absolutely was; this woman of his was stunning. He cupped the back of her head and angled her just as he needed so that he could tease and tempt a response. When her lips parted he speared his tongue inside, loving Hannah's taste.

The kiss changed, became more carnal. She gripped the sides of his head as she sucked his tongue, and gently raked it with her teeth. Max dipped his hand down from her waist to grip one firm globe of her ass and pull her tightly against him. Hannah moaned as she ground her pelvis against his erection. He thought his head might explode as this perfect lady turned to fire in his arms.

Max pulled his mouth from hers and sucked tiny kisses along her jaw to behind her ear, then swirled his tongue against the fragile skin. He'd always seen her rubbing that area when she was in deep concentration in front of her computer screen.

"Ahhhhhh," she moaned.

Max scraped his teeth against the hidden bundle of nerves, pulling her closer as she shuddered. He smiled as he took note of her sweet spot. He moved them down so they were sitting on her bed, and he started to unbutton her heavy silk blouse. Hannah trembled each time the backs of his fingers touched her flesh. God, she was so sensitive. When he got to the second-to-the-last button and his knuckles touched the satin flesh of her stomach she jerked in response. He looked at her face; her green eyes were practically black, and her flush went from the top of her breasts to the top of her cheekbones.

"Lie back," he said as he gently pushed her against her deliciously fragrant peach-colored sheets.

"Let me..." Her hands gestured toward him and he grinned. "Some other time. I'm the clothes-getter-off-er this morning."

Her eyelids shuttered to half-mast and she nodded. He pulled her blouse from the waistband of her gray slacks and unbuttoned the last two buttons. She sighed loudly with pleasure as his fingers traced upwards to flick open the front opening of her bra.

Hannah was going to be a noisy lover, how wonderful.

Max peeled back the cups of her bra and her breasts fell free into his waiting hands.

Coral.

Her nipples were coral.

He'd been dying to know that answer.

He pulled her into a sitting position so that he could get rid of the blouse and bra, then pulled off her socks, slacks, and panties. He chuckled when he saw how tightly she squeezed her thighs together.

"Uhmm," she looked down at herself, then looked up

at him and her eyes narrowed. "It's because you have all your clothes on. It's embarrassing."

Max laughed outright. "Good to know. I don't want you to be embarrassed," he teased.

It took less than a second for Hannah to start laughing too. She held out her arms for him and he put his knee beside her and went into her arms. "Kiss me," she coaxed.

"With pleasure."

As their kiss deepened, Max felt Hannah's fingers start to pull up his shirt. He pulled back from their kiss and stood up.

"Uh-uh. My job," he teased once again.

"Well, you're falling down on the job," she complained. Then it was Max's turn to flush as Hannah's eyes eagerly watched every bit of his flesh he uncovered.

She whimpered when he pulled off his boxers. And, thank the good Lord, her thighs parted.

Max circled one of her ankles and pulled it away from the other so that he could make room for himself between her legs. He took a good long look at the woman who was spread out before him.

"Uhmm," she whispered as she started to squirm.

"What?" he asked. He stroked both hands, from ankle to the top of her thighs, to her waist, and then cupped each full breast.

"What, Hannah?"

"You weren't doing anything," she mumbled as she arched upwards into his touch.

"Sure I was, I was surveying the terrain and determining the best way to approach." He sank down between her thighs, his cock resting against her leg as his mouth sucked one of her nipples in deep.

Hannah shouted his name and pulled his hair.

He rolled her other nipple between his thumb and forefinger, and then he groaned as she rubbed her silky thigh against his erection.

"Hannah, don't," he murmured. Up and down she slid against him, so silky, then she dipped her hand down and circled him and squeezed.

So fucking good!

Max pushed away from her nipples and her greedy hand. He slid down and pushed her thighs really wide then stroked his forefinger through her drenched slit.

"Damn," she moaned.

He pushed inside her as his tongue licked lazily around her swollen bundle of nerves at the apex of her sex. Hannah started to writhe against the sheets and Max stroked her stomach, trying to hold her down so he could ratchet up her passion.

"Max, quit playing," she growled and sank her fingers in his short hair. "For God's sake, fuck me already!"

He sucked her clit deep and she shrieked as her passage clamped around his finger.

Her glorious hair tossed against her pillow and her head shook from side to side as she climaxed. Max reared up and sheathed himself, then positioned his cock at her entrance.

"Yes," she begged.

He tried to move slow, he tried the best he could, but Hannah hooked her calf around his ass and pulled him in and he was lost.

"God yes," she hissed out as they started to merge. Her channel clenched around him and he started to sweat as he worked himself deeper. She was so tight.

"Am I hurting you?" He had to know.

"No," she affirmed. "You were made for me." Her arms

wound around his back, her legs gripped his ass as her pelvis pushed up, but it was still difficult for him to go deeper.

"Relax, Hannah," he soothed her with a soft kiss.

"I am relaxed," she snarled.

Max smiled and plunged further.

Almost.

So close.

He turned her head just a little and licked behind her ear and she shuddered. It was like turning a key in a lock—Hannah welcomed him home, and Max groaned. He waited as best he could before he began moving. She turned her head and caught him for another kiss. They were lost together as their bodies moved in an age-old rhythm that transcended time and space.

Max lifted his lips so he could look at Hannah's precious face. "I love you."

"Please let this last," she begged as their climax washed over them. Max knew what she meant, and he prayed that it would last too.

"Monkey sex?" Her mother asked as they got the dessert together to serve the three males in the dining room.

"Mom!" Hannah hissed.

"Just asking," Julie said with a butter-wouldn't-melt-in-her-mouth expression.

"Yeah, well, ask all you want, I'm not drinking any alcohol around you," Hannah promised them both.

"I'm thinking gorilla sex," Julie said primly as she cut into the pie.

"I swear to God," Hannah huffed as she slapped the

slice of lemon meringue pie onto the plate, "I will divorce you."

"You can't. It's not allowed in the Buffalo Grove Country Club bylaws." Julie smirked. Then her expression changed and she gave her daughter a serious look. "You haven't talked to me alone yet, not even a phone call. What's going on when it comes to potentially moving and Meghan's parents?"

Hannah gave her mom a guilty look. "I am so sorry. I have the biggest commission of my life and..."

"Yeah," Julie said wryly. "I know what the *and* is. I have one question, and it's serious, Honey. Does this look like you two might be moving together to Virginia as a couple?"

Hannah walked over to the kitchen doorway and saw that her dad was keeping Max and Zephyr entertained. She walked back to her mother. "God, I hope so. I'm so in love with him, I'm cross-eyed. Mom, he's as good a dad as Dad."

Julie's expression softened and she reached up and put her arm around Hannah's shoulders. "You know that in my heart, Zephyr is my first grandchild, but I sure wouldn't mind a couple more."

Hannah gulped.

"He talked about that," she whispered.

"I *knew* I liked that boy," Julie said fiercely.

Hannah snorted. "*Boy?*"

"That's what your father keeps calling him."

"Yeah, I know. I'm impressed Max keeps a straight face."

"One more reason I think he's wonderful." Julie dropped her arm and tidied up the pie that Hannah had messed up. "Okay, I think we can serve now."

18

"So still no repercussions?" Max asked Kostya.

"None except a reporter who I'm tempted to block."

Max chuckled. "Can I ask why?"

"Every damn time she hears about or reports on some humanitarian crisis, she has it in her head that my team is her personal Special Forces team to right the wrongs of the world."

Max laughed again.

"Not funny, Hogan. I just don't get it. I really don't. She's a smart, reasonable woman. She won a goddamn Pulitzer Prize for God's sake. She knows the real world. She knows how things work. When did she become so idealistic?"

Max opened his mouth to respond, then shut it. He thought about what Kostya said, and his tone of voice. He was really upset with Lark. Hell, not upset, this was hurting him. Max was pretty sure it was because Kostya felt like he was letting her down.

Max knew how it was for him and his team, all of them. They all had to learn how to compartmentalize their feelings about the things they saw and did; otherwise, they wouldn't survive. They were given orders and they had a job to do. They did the same thing that many front-line workers like doctors, the police, nurses, firefighters, and EMTs did. If they didn't do this, they'd be eaten alive in a heartbeat and not able to do their job.

"You're right, I've read Lark's stuff," Max agreed. "Hell, those reports of the people living in the shantytowns in Brazil were heartbreaking. Then add in how the gangs were targeting the kids? That stuff was raw."

"So what the fuck is wrong with her?" Kostya demanded to know. "Why has she changed? And why the hell is it spilling all over me?"

Max hesitated to tell him. It was all well and good when Kane kicked *his* ass, but he didn't know Kostya all that well. And what's more, if he *did* tell him, he was pretty sure Kostya *would* block her number. Max kind of thought Lark was good for him.

"Have you thought about confronting her about it?" Max asked.

"Shit, Hogan, I don't want another goddamn conversation with her. Another trip down another damn rabbit hole? I don't think so." Kostya sighed. "On another topic," his voice changed and there was a smile in it. "I saw the picture of your kid on the group text. How's that whole thing going? Did it blow your mind? What are you going to do?"

"Well, Kostya, I'm going to bring him home and raise him," Max laughed. "Isn't that what you would do?"

"Oh, well, yeah. Sure. Of course you would, except I heard he has like an aunt there in Chicago or something."

"No, the only family he has are his grandparents and they're abusive criminals. Meghan, his dead mother, had her best friend help raise him for the last year and a half of her life. She's going to be coming back to Virginia with me."

"Oh, that's good. Good for you, Max. Hey, I've got to get back to it; we've got a training exercise starting in a half-hour. Thanks for talking things through with me."

"Not a problem."

HANNAH DID her absolute best not to squirm in her seat as she and Max sat in front of Elias Peterson. God, how could this possibly be worse than the last time she was here?

But it is.

"I cannot believe that this hasn't just been thrown out on its ear," Elias said with absolute disgust.

He was shaking a thick set of legal-sized papers over his desk by his thumb and forefinger. "It's outrageous!"

"Elias, you're going to need to calm down," Max said in a soothing tone.

Hannah gaped at him. How in the hell could Max be looking so damned calm?

Hannah jerked to her feet. "Mr. Peterson, are you telling me that even though Max is now down as Zephyr's legal *father* those two assholes might have a chance in hell of getting custody of him!"

Elias dropped the legal brief onto his desk and held his hands outwards, trying to placate her. "Hannah, honey, take a breath."

"What kind of leg do they have to stand on?" she demanded to know.

"They're saying that Max here abandoned Meghan to die alone and that his job as a Navy SEAL proves he's an adrenaline junkie who is going to die early and will leave Zephyr an orphan again. They're saying they are Zephyr's most caring and stable option."

Hannah slammed her palms down on his desk. "That is a load of horseshit."

Max laughed and she swung around and yelled at him. "This is not fucking funny. They are the scum of the earth, and they will stop at nothing to get their hands on five fucking dollars, let alone a two million dollar life insurance policy."

Max tried to grab her hand and she jerked away from him. He would not be put off, so she let him pull her back down to her seat.

"Hannah, it's going to be okay. Kane has been pulling so much dirt on them that they are probably going to end up in jail."

She stopped and stared into his gray eyes. "Are you serious?"

"I am."

She looked over at the old lawyer. "Do you know about this?"

"Yes, Mr. Hogan has been giving me his information. He's assured me that he will be able to provide a proper chain of evidence that will satisfy law enforcement."

Hannah's eyes narrowed as she looked at Max. "What does that mean?"

"You're going to have to trust me. Can you do that?"

"But, Max, what happens if this goes to trial?" she whispered.

Elias cleared his throat and she turned back to look at him. "If Max can give me what he's shown me so far, it won't, Hannah."

Hannah tasted blood where she'd bit her lip. She turned back to Max and took a deep breath. "I trust you."

Max looked down at Hannah. The moon coming through the window made her look beautiful, but he hated seeing the purple smudges underneath her eyes. Tonight, she'd made love like it was her last night on earth. It wasn't until their third time together that she'd finally tumbled into a deep sleep.

He knew that she'd told him the truth in Elias' office this afternoon, she trusted him. But he'd lied. Right now none of Kane's findings could be given to the authorities with a proper chain of evidence, and what's more, even if they served up their crimes on a silver platter, nobody would stand as a witness.

Kane had been working on this with others; he and Kane knew that everything they had was the truth. They knew that Bob and Peggy Lancaster were filth, but it couldn't be proven in a court of law. Tonight he was going to have to make a decision.

He gave Hannah the softest of kisses, then slipped out of bed. He didn't want to be heard, so he took his phone and went down to her basement office, and shut the door.

Max swore that Kane picked up his call before it even rang.

"What in the hell took you so long to call?" Kane demanded to know. "I cannot fucking believe that Judge Reynolds is considering letting that fucking case go to fucking trial!"

"That was three 'fuckings' in one sentence. I'm not sure I want you around my kid," Max said evenly.

"I've created a secure server. It already has credible evidence on the money laundering that these two pieces of fuzzy toe mold perpetrated that can be corroborated by three different credible sources."

"Fuzzy toe mold?"

"Cullen said it once," Kane admitted. "It's sure as fuck is not my line. Did you hear me about the server and the evidence?"

"I fucking hate this," Max bit out. "By making you fabricate a bullshit crime so we can have credible evidence, your ass is swinging in the wind."

"The shit of it is, we're replicating the same damn thing they did before, Max, you gotta remember that," Kane rushed to reassure him.

"I get that. It still doesn't make it any less illegal."

"Jesus, Max, did you ask me to do a damn thing?" Kane demanded. "No. Hell, I had a copy of the brief that was filed *before* it was filed! I started creating this damned evidence *before* this brief was filed. There wasn't a chance in fucking, fucking, fucking hell I was going to let these two cocksuckers get anywhere near your son."

"And just for the fucking record. Dex, Gideon, and Clint are working on this with me, because I want this completed in forty-eight hours. I could take the time to get this done on my own before this thing goes to trial, no problem, but I don't trust the police to do the investigation on all this shit if I wait that long, even with it handed to them on a golden fucking platter. So I tapped all four SEAL teams. Every fucking one of those three men jumped at the chance. They fucking *jumped*. Do you hear me?"

Kane was not *practically* yelling into the phone. He *was*

yelling into the phone. In the eight years they'd worked together, Max had never heard him this angry.

He had to ask.

"Is everything okay with you?"

"Yes. Everything is fine with me. The team is great. But, Max, this is your son we're talking about. This would be like someone coming after Zed's daughter. The whole team goes batshit crazy when one of our women is targeted, but our women, they're fighters. But *our children*? Fuck no!"

Kane was absolutely right. It was how Max had felt since the first time he'd seen Zephyr. Hell, he agreed one hundred percent about little Lulu Zaragoza. He'd go balls to the wall to protect that little girl. He'd do *anything* for her, same as Zephyr.

"I'm going to send you how to access the server. I know you'll have to print everything out for the old guy."

"True," Max nodded. "So, are we having him give the stuff to the cops, the judge, or someone else?"

Kane hissed. "That's a sticking point. I finally had the time to investigate him. If this was thirty years ago, he'd be your man, he knew everyone. Now all of his friends are retired or dead. But, I ran into somebody in the hall earlier today who was talking about you and their personal problems. So, I made a call. I've got the perfect person."

"Who?"

"Lark. She knows fucking everybody. She can get all of this out in a heartbeat, and she knows how to get it out on the down-low."

Max felt the boulder that had been sitting on his chest finally roll off.

"I don't know how to thank you," Max breathed out.

"Fuck that shit, no thanks are necessary."

Max grinned. "You know, I'm pretty sure you said 'fuck' over twenty times. You're going to have to clean that up once I move Zephyr out there with me."

"Fuck, I'll have to get with Cullen." Kane gave a long-suffering sigh.

Max laughed even louder. He felt fucking great!

19

"How can you be so calm?" Hannah asked Max quietly, not wanting Zephyr to notice anything about her tone of voice since he was in the living room playing with his Hot Wheels.

"I'm calm because I'm putting a stamp on the last of Meghan's medical bills," Max said.

Hannah's eyes flared. "You know what I mean," she said as she stabbed her finger at Max's laptop. "Aren't you supposed to get the last of what you need for Mr. Peterson today?"

Max reached out and trailed his fingers down Hannah's arm. "Yes, I am. Don't worry, it's coming. You need to relax. I thought you were going to try meditating?"

"Meditating sucks donkey balls."

"Hannah, I'm serious, Gideon is going to get one more affidavit for me, and then I'll be printing it out and taking it over to Elias' office. It should be here within the next hour. After that, all of the evidence will be complete." Max pushed out his chair, grabbed her hand, and gave it a hard tug. Hannah fell easily into his lap.

"Zephyr will see," she protested even as she snuggled close.

"It's been over a month," he whispered in her ear. His teeth scraped behind her ear and the sensation caused her to melt.

"I hate those two people," Hannah whispered vehemently. They would have already had this house up for sale and been packing for Virginia if it weren't for Meghan's parents.

Max stroked his hand down the side of her body so that it rested on her hip, and then he gave her a gentle squeeze. "I'm doing something wrong if you're thinking about something other than this." His lips whispered against hers.

Once.

Twice.

Three times.

Hannah started following his mouth, wanting more than a tease, she wanted a taste.

She grabbed Max's head and pulled down so that she could kiss him properly. Not *too* properly, since Zephyr was in the other room, but enough for at least a sample. She swiped her tongue along Max's lower lip and gloried in his faint hum of approval. He squeezed her hip harder, and sparks shot directly into her feminine core.

Hannah went still. She so wanted to move against him. It took considerable effort not to squirm when she felt his hard erect flesh against her ass, but she stopped herself.

"You're right, Sweetheart," Max said as he rubbed his nose against hers. "We'll save this for tonight."

She looked into his dark gray eyes. "So what do you think?" he asked. "Was this more distracting than meditation?"

"Well, it didn't suck donkey balls."

THREE DAYS LATER, Max was shocked to find Lark Sorensen at the front door.

"Come on in out of the rain," he welcomed. "This is a surprise."

"Who's she, Dad?" Zephyr asked as he plowed into his leg and peeked around him to stare at Lark.

"She's a friend of mine, and you're going to have to move back away from the door with me so she can come inside."

Lark laughed. "It's so good to see you, Max. And who's this?"

He heard Hannah's footsteps coming up from the basement.

"Let me take your coat," Max offered. Lark handed it to him as Zephyr answered her question.

"I'm Zephyr Maxwell and now my last name is Hogan," he said proudly. "What's your name?" Hannah came to stand behind him as he looked up at Lark.

"I'm a friend of your dad's. My name is Lark Sorensen and I'm in town today just visiting some people so I thought I would come by and say hello."

Zephyr twisted his head to look from Lark to Max. "Is she one of the workers on your team?" he asked Max. "Is she a SEAL?"

Lark's laughter filled the room.

"No, son, she's not a SEAL. You'll meet my friends when we all move to my house in Virginia."

Zephyr twisted his head again, this time to look up at Hannah. "And you're coming too, right?"

Max grimaced. He wondered if there would ever come a day when Zephyr wouldn't need so much reassurance.

"Absolutely, I'm coming with you," Hannah grinned down at the boy. "But let's not forget our manners. We have a visitor, so why don't we ask Miss Lark to sit down and I get us all a drink, what do you think of that?"

Zephyr grabbed Hannah's hand. "Okay."

Max looked over at Lark and realized she hadn't missed one bit of the interaction, and knowing her, she knew exactly what it all meant. "Lark, before we head over to the living room, why don't you come over to the dining room and look over a couple of files I have, then we can get some drinks, how does that sound?"

"That sounds great," Lark said.

"Have you eaten anything?" Hannah asked Lark.

"I have dinner reservations with an old friend in two hours."

Hannah looked from Lark to Max, then down at Zephyr who was avidly watching all of the adults. "Hey, Zephyr, wouldn't it be cool if you helped me to get some cheese and crackers for everyone to go with the drinks?"

"Can we use squirt cheese?"

What is it with this kid and squirt cheese? That shit's disgusting.

"We'll see," Hannah said as she guided him to the kitchen.

"Ahhhhh," Zephyr whined as he followed her. "That always means no."

Lark laughed. "I pray to God that Taja and Nazy will sound exactly like your son does."

"Like a brat?" Max asked with a grin.

Lark beamed up at him. "Hell, Max, you know your kid is cute as hell. He's not a brat in the slightest, but he sure is outgoing and not afraid to ask for what he wants. That's what I want for the Nuri girls."

Max waved her toward the dining room table and pulled out a chair. "When did you last see Samira and the girls?"

"Two weeks ago. They are staying with a family in Santa Clara, near San Francisco. They're an older couple affiliated with a church who have been taking in refugees for decades. Mom made sure that this area has a strong Muslim community so that Samira would have a good network of people she and her girls could rely on."

"That's good," Max said with relief.

"That's my mom for you. She had that set up before we left Afghanistan."

Max gave Lark a close look. "So you and your mom are an awful lot alike, are you?"

"Not at all. I have no appetite for taking over the world," Lark snorted.

Max laughed. "Yeah, you only want to change it."

She gave him a disgruntled look. "Anyway, as I was starting to explain, they've already started attending English classes, and Samira found someone she once knew in Afghanistan at the community center. So far things are going really well."

Lark leaned over the table and pulled one of the manila files toward her. "Is this regarding our favorite duo?" she asked.

Max sat down next to her and whispered. "Zephyr's never met or heard about them, but I still don't want him to overhear anything about them, so let's not mention their names."

Lark nodded. Max opened the file. The first page was a printout with the three different crimes that were attributed to Bob and Peggy. Lark pointed to the top bullet point. "I went to Detective Roberts at the first district in Chicago. I bypassed Evanston's police department even though I have one contact there who is pretty solid, but she's only got four years on the force. Detective Roberts has worked twenty-two years as a detective, he doesn't want a promotion because he hates politics, all he wants to do is solve crimes."

"I like him already."

"So do I," Lark concurred. "He can sniff out bullshit a mile away, so this stuff better be bullet-proof."

"It is," Max assured her.

"I figured, because I already sent it to him. He wanted to meet with me in person; my guess is he wants to know my angle in all of this. He's my dinner date. I'm still trying to figure out what I'm going to say."

"Can't you just tell him the truth? Explain it's about me?"

Lark flipped through more pages. "I'm ninety percent sure that's what I'm going to say. I've been worried that if I bring your name up, and he knows you're a SEAL, he might realize that you could have someone doing some fancy footwork on the documentation."

Max grabbed another file and handed it to her. "Or, all my fancy footwork people spent their time gathering up all of this information..."

"I brung the can!" Zephyr shouted from the living room. "Hannah says that way if you want to squirt cheese on your cracker, you can."

"I think that is our cue to head in to join them," Max said.

"I love squirt cheese," Lark yelled out.

"See, Hannah, I told you," Zephyr practically jumped

up and down as Max and Lark entered the room. He ran over and handed Lark the can. "Do you need me to show you how it works?"

"That would be great," Lark grinned down at him. "Or better yet, maybe you could fix some crackers for me," she suggested.

Zephyr's eyes lit up.

"That was a mistake," Max muttered.

Max was rounding the turn to run back home. It was a miserable rainy day, and it matched his mood. He didn't give a shit if he was pushing himself, he intended to beat his best time since he arrived in Chicago. It had been nine days since Lark had visited, and neither Lark, Elias, or Kane had provided him an update on the status of Meghan's parents or the court case. He wanted those motherfuckers taken care of!

Simon had been great on the leave time, so that hadn't been a problem. His time with Zephyr and Hannah was pure pleasure, but Zeph had to sleep and Hannah had to work, and there was only so much HGTV a man could watch. When he thought his brain might atrophy, Simon had sent through a hellish old project his way. Apparently, the last time the SEAL team obstacle course had been completely overhauled was five years ago. Simon wanted to see at least five new obstacles employed by the time Max returned. Shit, this was an evil project, something that was better suited to Cullen Lyon's twisted brain, but Max loved it.

His feet sloshed through more mud puddles as he turned down the street to the old white house. Today was

Friday. *I'd better hear something today about the Lancasters* he thought as he made it to the front porch.

AFTER HIS HOT SHOWER, Max checked his phone. Kane had left a message to call him while he'd been in the bathroom.

"This better be good," Max growled into the phone.

"It is. Yesterday afternoon, warrants were approved for the Lancasters. This morning Bob was pulled out of a skeezy motel where he was found snorting coke off a prostitute's ass. They've got him down at the precinct being processed."

"And his wife?"

"They're still looking for her. She has a standing appointment at her favorite beauty salon this afternoon, so they expect to scoop her up then."

"And the charges? How comprehensive are they?" Max asked.

"Roberts did a fan-fucking-tastic job. If even half these charges stick, they're going down for fifteen years, at minimum."

"And their court case?"

"Gee, Max, I don't know how this could have happened, but somehow a copy of the arrest warrant got over to Wilma Demhurst, their attorney. She should be cutting them loose today."

Max paused. "You don't think she'll represent them, do you?"

"Not a chance in hell. The charges are solid, it would cost money to represent them. She's an ambulance chaser, she was only willing to go after Zephyr for a piece of the life insurance payout, even though that was illegal as hell. God knows what off-the-books kind of bullshit she was going to have to do to get them to give her a slice of that," Kane said with disgust.

Max slumped over where he was sitting on the bed. "So it's over?" he breathed out.

"Oh yeah, man. It's over. Now get your ass back home. I'm sick of leading this team of miscreants. They're a pain in my ass."

20

"It's going to be all right, Honey. Why do you look like you're going to cry?" Julie grabbed her daughter by her shoulders and pulled her in for a tight hug.

Hannah looked furtively over her shoulder, ensuring that Max and Zephyr were still loading the last couple of suitcases into her Dad's SUV as she and her mom watched the moving van drive down the street.

"I don't know," Hannah almost wailed as she tried to suck down the tears. She'd been a mess for the last three days. Fuck, she'd been so bad she thought it was her hormones so she just knew she was pregnant and was scared to death. Then she'd taken the pregnancy test this morning and when it had come up negative she'd lost her mind. She was so damned hurt and sad. Tears started falling again in front of her mom.

Julie looked at her and gave her another fierce hug, then yelled over her daughter's shoulder. "Hey, you, He-Men, I'm taking my baby to the airport in my car. You three can go to the airport in Chuck's car," Julie called out.

Max's head shot up as he closed the back of the SUV

and he started striding over to the two women. Hannah cringed.

"I've got this," her mother assured her, then marched toward the man she now considered a son.

Hannah watched as they met on the sidewalk in front of the old white house where Zephyr had spent the first years of his life. Max and Julie talked intently for a few quick minutes. Max looked up to stare at her a couple of times, then he finally nodded. Julie was smiling as she headed back to Hannah.

"Get into the car," she said as she came back to her. "You've got forty-five minutes to tell your Mama everything."

Hannah bit her bottom lip and thanked God for the woman who gave birth to her. She slipped into the passenger seat of the white Mercedes, then as soon as her mother barely stopped at the stop sign at the end of the street she began having second thoughts.

"Mom, I think I should drive."

"Nonsense. Your father has totaled his car twice, but I have never once had a traffic ticket, or a wreck." Her mother crossed into the left-hand lane without looking and the person behind them honked. Hannah looked up at the St. Christopher medal that her dad had attached to the visor and sighed.

"Now talk to me. I know that you are crazy in love. I know that in all ways but biology Zephyr is your son. So what's with the tears, Honey?"

"I don't know!" Hannah wailed. "Please help me. I'm begging you. I've got to get my shit together before I get on the plane."

"Take a breath, and just say what's in your heart," Julie said calmly.

Her Righteous Protector | 195

"What's deep in my heart of hearts is that I know I'm doing the right thing. *I know it.* Four months ago after Meghan died I wasn't sure that Zephyr would ever be okay again. I never thought I could make his world right. I was so scared."

Hannah slammed her eyes closed, remembering that solemn, mad, and grief-stricken little boy.

"But you did," her mother whispered as they came to a stoplight. She took Hannah's hand. "You did, Honey."

"No, I didn't," she protested. "Max did. I have never met anyone like him. He swooped in and made everything right in Zephyr's world. There is no way I could have done that."

And it hurt. It hurt so bad.

She took a deep, shuddering breath.

"Is that what's worrying you? That it's taking both of you to turn that little guy's life around?" Julie asked.

"Not only that, Mom. Max is making *my* life better. But what am *I* bringing to the table? I took a pregnancy test this morning."

Her mom hit her brakes.

"Mom! The light's green!"

"Sorry, dear," she continued on. "So are you pregnant?"

"No. But I wanted to be, I wanted it so bad. But am I just trying to tie us together before he finds out I'm not good enough for him?"

Julie gasped and took a fast right turn into a Target parking lot, then shut off the car. "Did I just hear you right?" she damn near shouted. "Where in the hell is this coming from? Are you not the woman who moved across the country to be with her dying friend, to help nurse her and raise her son? Are you not the woman who loved

Zephyr enough to make sure that he would have the best possible relationship with his father?"

Hannah nodded. She felt numb.

"Then why in the hell are you doubting yourself?"

"Mom, when I pictured a man I would marry, he was going to be boring. He was going to work beside me at some computer screen, and we would have sex twice a week, and two-point-five children. I wanted something safe."

Julie threw her an incredulous look. "Why in the hell would you have wished for that?"

Hannah's lip trembled. "After Clive, and all the people I saw pair off in L.A., that's what I wanted, especially, after watching Meghan die. I got so scared, Mom."

Julie grasped her hand and brought it to her lips. "I get that, Honey."

"I was doing really well with Max, I was, Mom. But then he blew me out of the water when he was able to literally vanquish Meghan's parents. Mom, he vanquished them like one of the superheroes from the movies I've worked on. How woo-woo is that? And he makes love like a superhero."

"Gorilla sex," Julie giggled.

"Shhhh, I'm serious. What's more, Zephyr looks up to him like a superhero..." Hannah's voice trailed off.

"So why is any of this a problem?"

"It won't last?" she asked. "I don't deserve it? I don't know, Mom, choose one. All I can say is that I'm scared as hell."

"Hannah Rebecca Woods, you just listen to me. I raised you to be the superhero in your own story. When in the world did you forget that? When did you get scared? I have watched both Zephyr and Max look at you like the sun rises and sets on you. You love Max, don't you?" Julie asked.

"With my whole heart."

"And Zephyr?"

Hannah rolled her eyes. "Get real," she said.

"Then wake up and smell the coffee. You are starting the biggest and brightest adventure of your damned life! You're a superhero right along with Max."

Hannah looked into her mother's wise eyes and felt herself begin to calm down.

"You're right," she whispered.

"Well, of course I'm right."

"No," Hannah said louder. "I mean you're exactly right."

Julie rolled her eyes and started the car. "Let's get going, you have a plane to catch."

MAX LOOKED over at Hannah as they sat in the backseat of Zed's SUV. He was the team member who had a car seat for Zephyr, so he was who picked them up from the airport.

"The house is kind of small compared to what you're used to," Max whispered above Zephyr's sleeping head.

Hannah gave him an angelic smile. "Honey, you've only mentioned that ten times since we've landed. For goodness sakes, somehow you've managed to show me a floorplan with dimensions, I know what the house is like." She reached past Zephyr's feet and held out her hand so he could hold it. Max grabbed it like a lifeline. Whatever Hannah's mom had said to her on the way to the airport had turned his woman into a new person—confident and fearless. Or maybe he was seeing the real Hannah at last, now that they were past their troubles. He felt like they'd traded places—he was the worried one now and she was his rock.

Max looked up to the front seat where Zed was driving. He'd noticed that Zed hadn't been saying a thing since they'd gotten on the highway from the airport. He must have picked up on how anxious Max was. As they got closer to his house, Max started calming down. He realized that his neighborhood was kind of like the older neighborhood that Meghan's house had been in. He'd been keeping in touch with Lester and Mikey, so they'd be expecting all of them in a few days. There would be that to look forward to.

Max frowned when he looked down the block.

Dammit!

He caught Zed's eyes in the rearview mirror and his expression was totally blank, which was such total bullshit.

"Zaragoza," he growled softly, not wanting to wake Zephyr before they had to.

Hannah's hand tightened on his.

"What is it?" she asked.

When Zed stopped his vehicle in front of his house, Max saw the new cedar fence that now stretched out on either side of his house. He would bet a hell of a lot of money that it enclosed his entire backyard.

"Somebody better have kept receipts," he snarled.

"Don't worry," Zed gave a long-suffering sigh. "Asher insisted that Kane start a spreadsheet along with all of the receipts scanned in for you to look at."

"Are we here?" Zephyr asked as his head lifted. He looked first at Hannah and then at Max.

Hannah was grinning—of course she had figured out what was going on. She was always quick on the uptake.

"Yes, Honey, we're here," Hannah said.

Zephyr worked the straps off the car seat and started to wiggle out. "Do I get to see my bedroom? How close are we to the beach? Do I get to meet Mikey? When are Grandma Julie and Grandpa Chuck going to visit? Are all your friends as big as Mr. Zed?"

Max picked Zephyr up out of the seat and walked around to the other side of the SUV to open Hannah's door, but she already had it open. He grabbed her hand. "Let's go see what other damage they've done," he grumped.

Hannah peeked over at Zed. "So you guys have been busy, huh?"

Zed walked in front of them and used a set of keys to open the front door. "We got bored," he shrugged. "Well, Cullen did, but he has ADHD. We'd really been hoping when he married a doctor she'd prescribe something for him, but no such luck."

Zed stepped back, allowing Hannah to walk into the house first. "Max, it's gorgeous."

Gorgeous? Fuck, what had they done?

He peered over her head.

Holy hell, they knocked out a wall!

It was now open between the tiny kitchen and living room, and those damned bastards had installed French doors out to the backyard. They'd painted all the walls cream with light blue trim. Which of their women had helped with that? Hell, the whole place was open and filled with light!

"Ohhhh, there is a bouquet of flowers, did you do

that?" Hannah sighed as she went over to the dining room table and pulled out the card.

It was a big card. He watched her read it.

"There are a lot of names."

Zephyr wiggled out of his arms. "Where's my room?" he demanded to know.

"Uhmmmm," Max started.

"Go look, I'll bet you'll figure it out," Zed said with a grin.

Max stared at his friend. "You guys are too much," he said as Hannah looked at the card. As he suspected it contained all the members of his team and their women.

"How am I going to memorize all of them?" Hannah fretted.

Then she looked around the room. "We're going to have to invite them all over."

Zed put a reassuring hand on her shoulder. "Hannah, don't worry about it, truly. None of us ever entertain at our house. Kane's a rich son of a bitch, and he has the show house to prove it. We invite ourselves over there and force him to buy food and barbeque. We're already planning a welcome home party after you get settled."

"Hannah! Dad! I have a racecar bed! Come look! And a Chicago Bears poster! And a picture of the ocean! Dad, is that a picture of you?" Zephyr shouted as he ran back out to the living room and grabbed at Max's arm.

"You have to come look at my room, Dad. You've got to."

Max laughed. "Hold on a second, I'll be right there."

"Okay, but hurry, Dad."

Then he turned to Hannah and practically dragged her out of the room as she laughed all the way down the hall. Zephyr was talking a mile a minute.

"God, Zed, I never understood it before," Max said, his voice filled with awe as he looked at his long-time friend.

"Having a family, or when he calls you Dad?"

"Both," Max breathed out. "It cracks my heart wide open."

"Me too. Welcome to the club."

21

"*Clara's Galaxy*," Zephyr begged.

Thank God she'd remembered to pack that in the luggage that she'd taken on the plane. She opened the book so she could start 'reading' it to Zephyr.

"This bed is not great for storytime," Max grumbled again. He'd brought in two of the dining room chairs so that he and Hannah could read to Zephyr because the racecar bed had plastic sides that didn't allow for them to sit on it with him.

Hannah shook her head at him in exasperation.

"You love your bed, don't you Zeph?" she asked the boy.

"It's awesome!"

Hannah looked down at the book and started to make up the story. Max knew that Dickerson's next installment would be out soon, and Zephyr would be wanting that book instead. He wondered what kind of story Hannah would make up for that book.

He waited impatiently for Zephyr to fall asleep. You would have thought with all of the excitement of the day that he'd be out like a light, but nope, Hannah had to read the whole damn thing before he started his little boy snores.

By the time they closed his door and put on the baby monitor, Hannah was giving Max the side-eye.

"What?" she finally asked as they made it into his bedroom.

"What do you mean what? You were the one who needed all the alone time with your mom today. You scared the living shit out of me. For a moment there I thought you were going to bail on me."

Hannah gaped at him. "You're not serious," she exclaimed as she grabbed him around the waist. "Max, I adore you." She shoved his T-shirt up and he stayed her hands, then cupped her cheeks.

"Hannah, you haven't been talking for three days. I tried to get you to open up. Then I found the negative pregnancy test. Why didn't you tell me you were worried about that? You should know you can talk to me about anything. I would love it if we had a child together. I want us to last forever, I told you that."

Her beautiful green eyes filled with tears.

"I'd been feeling like I didn't measure up," she whispered hoarsely.

Max shook his head. "I don't understand."

Hannah blew out a big breath and stared up at him. He felt himself relax because he could see...he saw the love shining out her eyes.

Thank fuck!

"Part of me felt guilty, and that's what the tears have been about, because I was getting my every dream come true—because of Meghan. But then part of me feels like she gave you to me. You know? It's like she threw you away, but then wrapped you up in a bow and gave you to me. At least that was what I finally decided on the plane. But before that, I'm telling you, I was a mess," she sighed. "Mom made me figure out a lot of it."

Max smiled gently. He loved Meghan's mom. "What did she make you figure out?"

"That I deserved you. That I deserve happiness, and to be the hero of my own story."

"She's right," he whispered.

He whisked her T-shirt over her head. "What else do you deserve?" he asked as he looked into her eyes, and his fingers unclipped her bra.

Hannah palmed the front of his jeans, she stroked his erection.

"She said I deserved gorilla sex."

"Huh?"

"Take off your clothes, Max, and I'll show you."

Hannah was nervous as she walked out onto the big deck at Kane's gorgeous home. It was filled with people. The last time she'd been at a party this big, it had been in L.A., and she'd hated those.

"Hey, Max!" Kane shouted from the barbeque. "Glad to have you back." She'd met him a few times when he'd come over to their house.

Every face on the deck turned to them. They all saw Zephyr in Max's arms, and they didn't swarm—they were all too smart for that—for which Hannah was greatly appreciative.

Zed broke apart from the crowd. He was carrying the cutest little girl. She had dark curls like Zephyr's, big brown eyes, and she was wearing all pink and fairy wings. A beautiful woman was walking beside them.

"Hiya, Mr. Zed," Zephyr called out from the safety of his father's arms. Both children studied one another, then the girl whispered into her father's ear.

"Zephyr, I'd like to introduce you to my daughter, Lulu."

"Hiya, Lulu," Zephyr smiled. He wiggled and Max put him down. "Can you fly?" he asked Lulu.

"Oh God," her mother said.

Zed set her down.

"Remember what I told you," her mother warned her.

She shoved her fists on her hips and frowned up at her mother. "I remember," she said with a pout. *She's adorable*, Hannah thought.

"Lulu," Zed's voice contained a low warning.

"Fine, I can't jump off things. I might get hurt," she huffed.

"I will take your wings away from you," the woman said matching her child's huff.

Hannah heard Max's cough that was clearly covering a laugh.

"Dad, can I have wings?" Zephyr asked.

"No!" Max and Hannah said simultaneously.

"Let's go into the kitchen," Lulu said. "Miss A.J. said I could help ice cupcakes. Wanna help?"

"Can I lick the spoon?" Zephyr asked Lulu.

"Only after I do."

"Zephyr, use a different spoon, okay?" Hannah called after the little boy as he ran after Lulu back into the house.

"Why in the hell did you buy her those wings?" the little woman growled at Zed.

"Hi, Hannah, let me introduce you to my wife, Marcia," Zed smiled at Hannah. She smiled and held out her hand to Hannah.

"Let me show you around. Kane's barbecuing; it's his house," Marcia explained.

"I met him. I also met A.J. when we came in."

"Then let me introduce you to some of the others. They're great."

Hannah followed her into the crowd, feeling more confident about meeting all of Max's friends.

MAX LOOKED around the table at his friends. Hannah was across the table from him and Zephyr was asleep in his lap. How was it that every day just kept getting better?

A.J. and Hannah were in an intense conversation. It turned out that they actually knew some of the same people since they'd both lived in L.A. Who would have guessed? It was good to see her so relaxed and enjoying herself, fitting right in with all the rest.

Again, better and better.

"So, are you ready to get back to work on Monday?" Cullen asked him.

"So ready," Max answered.

Cullen looked down and gave a piercing look to Zephyr.

"He's out like a light, Max assured him. "Say whatever you want."

"Have you talked to Hannah about leaving on missions?"

"Yeah, I have. Hannah's been through hell and back in

her own life with Meghan; she knows that life isn't always fair. We have the same philosophy, thank God."

"What's that?" Cullen asked.

"You have to grab hold and suck every bit of joy out of life that you can, for as long as it lasts."

Cullen looked across the table at Max's woman and a smile spread across his face. "You've got a good one."

"I know. I know I do." Max agreed.

EPILOGUE

"Your dad promised me ice cream a long, long, long, long time ago," Mikey said as he got into the backseat of Max's Cougar. It had taken some doing, but Zephyr's car seat was safely installed in the backseat. Both Mikey and Zephyr were wearing matching smiles and Chicago Bears jackets.

Now that they were finally ensconced in the backseat, he turned to Hannah. "Your chariot awaits." He held out his hand to help her into the front seat.

"It's not a chariot, Max, it's a Mercury Cougar," Mikey corrected, his voice filled with disdain. Max chuckled as he walked around the front of the car.

"Dad, how come again there isn't any roof on your car?" Zephyr asked when Max got behind the wheel.

"It's a convertible," Mikey told Zephyr patiently. He'd been really patient and kind with Zephyr all day. "He took off the roof for me."

Max hadn't driven his Cougar with the top down with Zephyr in the car yet. He'd been waiting to do it when he had them both together. He wanted it to be a treat.

Zephyr looked over at Mikey with awe. "Can we play Hot Wheels again when we get back to your house?"

"Yep. After ice cream. Remember, we can't eat it in your dad's car. That's a rule."

"Is everybody ready?" Max asked.

He received a chorus of 'yeses.'

He looked over at Hannah, who looked gorgeous. He couldn't resist, so he leaned over and gave her a long, lush kiss.

"Ick," two voices yelled from the back seat.

"They do that a lot," Zephyr informed Mikey.

"I think that means they're in love," Mikey told Zephyr. "They should get married."

Max lifted his lips from Hannah's just a fraction and looked into her beautiful green eyes.

"We're going to, you know," he whispered.

She raised her eyebrows.

"Get married. We're going to get married. We're going to have more children. And every day is going to get better and better and better. I love you, Hannah Woods."

"Oh, Max, I love you too." She brushed her thumb against his lip. "You're my superhero."

READ KOSTYA *and Lark's exciting stand-alone story in Caitlyn's new Navy SEAL series coming out in January, 2021. The book is called* **Her Selfless Warrior**.

ABOUT THE AUTHOR

Caitlyn O'Leary is a USA Bestselling Author, #1 Amazon Bestselling Author and a Golden Quill Recipient from Book Viral in 2015. Hampered with a mild form of dyslexia she began memorizing books at an early age until her grandmother, the English teacher, took the time to teach her to read -- then she never stopped. She began re-writing alternate endings for her Trixie Belden books into happily-ever-afters with Trixie's platonic friend Jim. When she was home with pneumonia at twelve, she read the entire set of World Book Encyclopedias -- a little more challenging to end those happily.

Caitlyn loves writing about Alpha males with strong heroines who keep the men on their toes. There is plenty of action, suspense and humor in her books. She is never shy about tackling some of today's tough and relevant issues.

In addition to being an award-winning author of romantic suspense novels, she is a devoted aunt, an avid reader, a former corporate executive for a Fortune 100 company, and totally in love with her husband of soon-to-be twenty years.

She recently moved back home to the Pacific Northwest from Southern California. She is so happy to see the seasons again; rain, rain and more rain. She has a large fan group on Facebook and through her e-mail list. Caitlyn is known for telling her "Caitlyn Factors", where she relates her little and big life's screw-ups. The list is long. She loves hearing and connecting with her fans on a daily basis.

Keep up with Caitlyn O'Leary:

Website: www.caitlynoleary.com
FB Reader Group: http://bit.ly/2NUZVjF
Email: caitlyn@caitlynoleary.com
Newsletter: http://bit.ly/1WIhRup

- facebook.com/Caitlyn-OLeary-Author-638771522866740
- twitter.com/CaitlynOLearyNA
- instagram.com/caitlynoleary_author
- amazon.com/author/caitlynoleary
- bookbub.com/authors/caitlyn-o-leary
- goodreads.com/CaitlynOLeary
- pinterest.com/caitlynoleary35

ALSO BY CAITLYN O'LEARY

OMEGA SKY SERIES
Her Selfless Warrior (Book #1)
Her Unflinching Warrior (Book #2)

NIGHT STORM SERIES
Her Ruthless Protector (Book #1)
Her Tempting Protector (Book #2)
Her Chosen Protector (Book #3)
Her Intense Protector (Book #4)
Her Sensual Protector (Book #5)
Her Faithful Protector (Book #6)
Her Noble Protector (Book #7)
Her Righteous Protector (Book #8)

NIGHT STORM LEGACY SERIES
Lawson & Jill (Book 1)

THE MIDNIGHT DELTA SERIES
Her Vigilant Seal (Book #1)
Her Loyal Seal (Book #2)
Her Adoring Seal (Book #3)
Sealed with a Kiss (Book #4)
Her Daring Seal (Book #5)
Her Fierce Seal (Book #6)

A Seals Vigilant Heart (Book #7)
Her Dominant Seal (Book #8)
Her Relentless Seal (Book #9)
Her Treasured Seal (Book #10)
Her Unbroken Seal (Book #11)

BLACK DAWN SERIES
Her Steadfast Hero (Book #1)
Her Devoted Hero (Book #2)
Her Passionate Hero (Book #3)
Her Wicked Hero (Book #4)
Her Guarded Hero (Book #5)
Her Captivated Hero (Book #6)
Her Honorable Hero (Book #7)
Her Loving Hero (Book #8)

THE FOUND SERIES
Revealed (Book #1)
Forsaken (Book #2)
Healed (Book #3)

SHADOWS ALLIANCE SERIES
Declan

Made in United States
North Haven, CT
12 April 2024